Defender
of
Freedom

Clifton LaBree

© 2017 by Author, Clifton LaBree

Published by
Fading Shadows Imprint
New Boston, New Hampshire, USA

Paperback ISBN-13: 978-1-943329-33-5
EBook ISBN-13: 978-1-943329-34-2

Cover Design by Vivian LaBree
Front Cover Picture: New Hampshire State Veterans Cemetery
Boscawen, NH, USA

This book is a work of fiction. The characters are fictional, but the historical events and dates have been seriously researched and are factually presented. Any resemblance to actual persons is entirely coincidental.

Dedicated to my wife Pauline, and my family, with thanks for all their support and encouragement.

Chapter One

American soldiers arrived in France in 1918. The war against Germany was going badly for the Allies. After four years of bloodshed, the Allied and German soldiers were on the verge of exhaustion and collapse. The cocky Yanks were determined to show the world that they were not so consumed with soft living that they could not fight. They were innocent and had a lot to learn, but they were also eager to do their part.

By mid-1918 the powerful German Army was poised for an assault on Paris. If successful, the attack would mean the end of the war. The Allied command worried that they could not stop a determined German effort to capture Paris. The future looked grim! After years of painful attrition, despair and defeatism were commonplace.

At this low point in morale, the intrepid Americans were given a decisive section of their own at the front most threatened by the German advance toward Paris. Within days the inexperienced American divisions had challenged the enemy with a ferocity and determination that brought the German momentum to a halt. The Allies witnessed the Yanks defeat one of the strongest European armies ever put into the field, and they did it with an élan and valor that won the admiration of nations around the world.

The American citizen-soldiers even surprised themselves. It had taken them a while to adjust to combat, for they were inexperienced and poorly equipped for war. Likewise, the casualties they suffered during their first few days had shattered any preconceived notions of warfare. A difficult emotional adjustment was required of them as well. However, the American doughboy was famous for his resourcefulness, and adapted to various military situations quicker and more effectively than most of the European troops because they were not hindered by inflexible traditions.

Despite the phenomenal odds against them, they marched to the front with an air of invincibility in stark contrast to the French and British soldiers, whose units had suffered untold brutalities in frontal assaults that had accomplished nothing for the Allied cause. Consequently, the Allied soldiers no longer believed that their cause could be won; they had simply seen and been through too much. Despite their deeply entrenched cynicism, they were encouraged by the determination and willingness of the Yanks to close with the Germans. Morale was quickly boosted, and the Allied cause seemed reborn with a new sense of nobility and honor. When the French high command warned the American forces that they wouldn't be able to halt the Germans, the Yanks collectively shrugged their shoulders and proceeded to stop the enemy everywhere the lines were held by American soldiers. They saved Paris for future generations and rekindled the prospect of victory when it had seemed unattainable just a short time before.

The United States entered the conflict because it was a just and righteous cause. The untried Yanks had crossed the cold Atlantic to fight a type of war they knew little about. American citizen-soldiers had marched to war in defense of liberty and freedom for all of mankind, asking nothing for their heavy sacrifices. They were like a breath of fresh air to the war-weary peoples of France and Belgium, bringing hope where there was despair and victory where there was stalemate and defeat. The American Army had established a standard of excellence admired by the rest of the world. It was a monumental feat especially since the Army had been little more than a constabulary force in settling the American west. It was a selfless act of charity by the American people unequaled by any other nation in the world, and their contribution was decisive.

A weary mud-splattered Captain Emile Ranta carefully lit the lamp above the field desk to illuminate the stack of papers he had to process that evening. The sound of artillery continued into the dark night belching its fiery destruction towards the hill that the Captain's infantry company had just wrested from the

Germans and occupied before it got dark. It had been a vicious battle with German and American soldiers fighting hand-to-hand until there was no longer a will to continue by the Germans. It was a bloody victory that had taken over half of his company. He wept openly when he saw the large number of soldiers he had lost in the span of a few hours.

After establishing proper lookout points around the hilltop for any German movement against their defense lines, Emile placed a helmet full of name tags from the dead soldiers of his company on his field desk. Tears filled his eyes and ran down over his grimy face. He had sustained over forty percent casualties in the past twenty-four hours.

He was interrupted by Second Lieutenant John Courtland, a young commander of first platoon. He too was covered with mud and grime and had a traumatic expression on his face. "I don't have enough men to cover the east flank, Captain. I've lost seventy percent of my platoon in just three hours of combat," he exclaimed, wiping his face with his dirty shirtsleeve, and collapsing in the chair offered by Emile. They both stared out the tent opening at the artillery flashes in the darkness.

"It's going to be a long night, John. Your platoon performed magnificently. As usual, intelligence was wrong about the German forces facing the hill, and we paid the price for the lack of adequate information," Emile told him, knowing exactly what the young officer was going through. He had been in that same place earlier in his tenure when they first entered the fight.

"What about the perimeter defenses, Captain?"

"I'll give you all of the replacements we have available. Tell the operations officer to release them to your platoon and do the best you can pairing the green troops with men who have already experienced combat. I wish I could do better, John. I'll see if regiment can help us out in the morning."

John started out the door and turned to ask, "If the positions become untenable, do I have permission to pull back to our starting line?"

Emile prayed that he would never have to give the order he gave to John. "Lieutenant, I have specific orders from battalion and regiment that this position must be held, regardless of the cost..."

John swallowed hard and saluted, "I understand, Sir."

Emile had a sick feeling that he had just handed a death sentence to John and what was left of his platoon. He watched him walk out the opening in the tent. The high price paid for a small hill in the middle of a flat plain was incomprehensible. Soon telegrams would be received in homes all across the country notifying them of the death of their loved ones. The battle waged by grieving mothers and sweethearts was every bit as intense and bitter as those fought on the battlefield. They suffered in the silence of their homes and lifted their eyes to the Heavens asking why? Nothing helped to ease their pain and anguish. They mourned alone in silence.

As intense as the pain was for those at home, Emile carried the same pain in his heart. The only difference was that he mourned for hundreds and was constantly searching to determine if he might have done something different to ease the cost. "Hold at all cost" was a cruel command that he would carry to his grave.

Ultimately the hill had been captured and now they were prepared to take casualties defending it. The Germans always mounted a counter attack whenever they were overrun. They fought with a tenacity equal to the Americans who were late in joining the Allied cause on the battlefield. French and British forces were worn out and discouraged, and they were losing to the determined German drive toward Paris.

The inexperienced American Army had positioned themselves in front of the Germans to block their advance. They brought to the battlefield a fresh willingness to close and defeat the enemy. The unique stand of the Americans was working, but the price was high, combat losses were heavy. Their taciturn stand amazed the French and the British who had predicted that they could not stop the German drive. The vicious struggle lasted for several weeks.

Each day, Emile had lost count of them, was more difficult than the previous one. He was exhausted and wondered when the insanity would end. He had lost John Courtland and most of his platoon defending their hilltop positions. The small knoll in the middle of open land had been heavily contested, but the Americans held their positions. Reinforcements sent by regiment made the difference. The German's offensive on their eastern front was stopped, and they no longer tried to take the hill.

For four days and nights Emile's company had defended the hill against everything the Germans could throw against them. On the fourth day, a courier motorcycle rider appeared at the command post with a package of mail and current dispatches. He ran into the tent and saluted Captain Ranta. "I have a dispatch for you that has just been issued all along the front, Sir," he stated firmly, placing a packet with a manila folder on Emile's desk. "The orders are to cease fire and hold in place until further orders."

Emile heard the words but it took a while for them to register on his weary mind. "Are you sure, Corporal?"

"Yes, Sir. I've got to complete my rounds. It sure looks like the real thing. Only time will tell."

"Thanks, son," Emile said, eagerly opening the dispatch and read:

TO ALL ALLIED COMMANDS AT THE FRONT

November 10, 1918

You are hereby ordered to cease fire immediately upon the receipt of this order. You are ordered to hold in place being alert for any violations of this order being simultaneously sent to Allied and German commands. As soon as the official documents are agreed upon you will be notified. Report any violations to this order to your command center. If you are threatened by the enemy, you have permission to defend yourselves. The call is yours.

Further orders will be forthcoming. We pray that this is the moment we have all been looking for.

Emile immediately called for an officer conference to order the ceasefire to be spread to all of the outposts. When the officers filed into the tent, there was an air of uncertainty present. As soon as he read the dispatch, loud and enthusiastic cheers filled the air.

"Okay men, get out there to pass the word. Hold in place means just that. Tell the men to be optimistic, yet they should be on the lookout for any mischief the Germans may have in mind. I want to know as soon as possible of any violations of the order. Understood?"

"Yes, Captain Ranta," the group replied in unison, rushing out the opening of the tent to spread the good word.

Emile smiled, sitting alone at his desk. He was pleased to hear of the potential armistice, but he was practical enough to know that anything could happen to change the situation. The heavy losses he had sustained just prior to the ceasefire made him physically sick. He walked to the opening in the tent listening to the shouts and cries of thanksgiving from the men. He had a strange feeling that something was missing, and he realized it was the lack of artillery gunfire. The silence was deafening. Rarely had there ever been more than a few minutes of each day without some kind of gunfire, either Allied or German, dominating the battlefield. The noise accompanied by flashes of explosions had been such a constant component to their environment that they were slow to adapt to the eerie silence of the muddy battlefield.

Listening carefully in the darkness, Emile could hear distinct sounds from the German trenches just over the lip of the hilltop. They too were thankful for the cessation of fighting. They were weary and sickened by the killing and maiming of soldiers on both sides. Warriors of every description shared the same feelings. He was warned to be on the alert for any German violation of the temporary truce to better their bargaining position at the armistice table. The killing had stopped, and both sides took advantage of the moment to take better care of their wounded and dead comrades. The time also generated thoughts of home and loved ones. Maybe now there was a chance that they really could return home without being wounded or killed. The dreams were universally held by all of the warriors.

The view from the tent was that of total desolation and destruction. Nothing remained on the landscape except occasional stubs of tree trunks standing as charred sentinels in the midst of a land plowed into pulverized muddy morasses mixed with remnants of buildings and body parts of those unfortunate soldiers who were at ground zero of an artillery shell.

Sergeant Jeff Ordway saw his company commander standing motionless in the opening of the command tent and joined him. "I hope this is the real thing, Captain."

"You speak for all of us, Sergeant. I never expected to see it come so quickly once the Germans began their march towards Paris. Our American forces have made a difference once we were given a section of the line that was our responsibility." Emile filled his pipe with tobacco. He knew that Jeff Ordway was a pipe smoker, too. "Here, Jeff, try some of this burley tobacco. It's mild and sweet."

"Thanks, Captain. At times like this, a good pipe is a comfort. I've been thinking a lot about home lately. I hope my family has put up enough firewood for the winter. Our Maine winters are a little more severe than this section of France. My, how I miss home."

Jeff and Emile were both from Monson, Maine. Jeff had been a part of the Maine National Guard company with Emile as their commander. They had stayed together all during their training sessions in France. They were good friends. Jeff was older than Emile and was proud that his friend had risen to the rank of Captain. He never took advantage of their friendship to obtain special treatment, and Emile appreciated that.

Emile took a puff from his pipe with a solemn expression on his face and said, "The last letter from my wife, Bonnie, was a little frightening. Several people in town have died from the dreaded flu epidemic that has spread across the entire country. Have you heard from your family, Jeff?"

"My letters from home haven't mentioned any family members that have had the disease. Thank God for that. I understand that more people at home have been killed by the flu than have been killed here in action by the Germans."

"I can believe that," Emile replied. "What are you going to do if this is the real thing, Jeff? We'll be sent home shortly I'm sure. We were the first to be shipped to France and should be the first to go home."

"I may go back to the slate quarries where I started right after school. Going into the pulp camps for Great Northern Paper Company is a good job for someone single like me. It's a chance to save money for most of the winter. When the spring drive comes and the choppers leave the woods for home, you get paid all of your earnings at once. Some men come out of the woods and get drunk and gamble away all their wages in a few days. I'd like to use one winter salary to go to school for a trade. Every one in town was proud that you went to college and became a forester. Are you going to stay in the Army or go to work somewhere as a forester?"

"I haven't made up my mind yet, Jeff. Ever since you and I joined the National Guard, I've enjoyed serving in the Army. I think it depends a lot on Bonnie. It would be hard for her if I stayed on after we leave France. She doesn't like being alone, and I can't blame her."

"Well, I better get back to the squad. I noticed that our new platoon leader had a field kitchen moved into our bivouac area. Pretty soon we'll have hot coffee and warm bread, Captain. When it's ready, I'll see that you get some," Jeff said, turning to leave.

"Thanks, Jeff. It will be appreciated, the night has a damp feel to it. I don't expect it, but have your men be on the alert for a German counter attack."

"I'll pass it on, Captain."

The night passed without incident. The next day it rained, turning the land into sticky quagmires of pulverized mud. The soldiers were hard pressed to find enough firewood to maintain their campfires. The cold rain penetrated to their bones. The field kitchen was the most popular location. Hot coffee and bread were consumed as soon as it was ready. Emile was on his third mug of coffee eating a thick slice of warm bread and jelly, when a courier rode up beside the kitchen and turned off his Indian motorcycle.

"Your company is fortunate to have a field kitchen, Captain Ranta," the courier said, pouring himself a cup of coffee from a large urn on the hot plate. "That tastes good. I have some mail for your company and a packet of dispatches for you, Sir. Every company commander is receiving notice that a formal armistice will take place tomorrow at 1100 hours. The Germans have agreed to surrender…"

Chapter Two

Emile was expecting notification of a formal surrender. Once the words from the courier sunk in, he was speechless. His first emotion was that he would not be going home a cripple and Bonnie did not have to suffer the trauma of knowing that he had been killed... Suddenly the future looked bright with expectations! He tore open the dispatch and read it with a lump in his throat.

> This bulletin is to inform you that the German High Command and the Allied Central Command have agreed on the terms in which the German Army will surrender to the Allied forces. All necessary documents have been signed by all parties. The official surrender will take place at 11:00 AM, November 11, 1918, across the entire battlefield.
>
> Any violations of this painfully crafted document will be severely condemned.
>
> It is suggested that any wounded men, German or Allied, who have not been treated, should be cared for immediately.

Emile looked at his watch, passing the document to the executive officer of the company for posting on the bulletin board. "Pass the word down the line that in twenty minutes the war will officially be over."

He knew that this time would come eventually, but he was not in a mood to rejoice. Images of good men lost who were not going home clouded his thoughts. He looked at the mail pouch and had the contents delivered to the platoons for distribution. He had a letter from his wife, Bonnie, and hurriedly opened it.

My Darling Husband,

Tonight is a sad one for me. I am having trouble finding the correct words to inform you that your mother has passed away. The flu epidemic has hit the town causing untold despair to our small community. Your father worked tirelessly when your mother came down with the dread disease. Nothing seemed to help. So far we've lost twenty people in town.

I feel so sad for you who have been facing death on the battlefield and now must come face to face with it in our family. I pray for you every night my love. May God shield you from harm and bring you home to us soon.

The papers are full of news about Germany's push against Paris. It seems as if the world is tearing itself apart and you are right in the middle of the conflict.

The day you come home to my arms will be the happiest of my life. Goodnight. I send my love to you via the beautiful harvest moon that is out tonight.

Love,

Bonnie

Emile placed the letter on his desk with trembling hands. His mother was gone and he never had a chance to say goodbye or to tell her how much he loved her kind and caring ways. He could imagine the terrible time his beloved father was having. Their love and respect for each other had created a warm and loving atmosphere for him to grow up in. He laid his arms on the desk and wept, feeling alone and helpless.

His grief was interrupted by the sudden ringing of church bells nearby. The compound was alive with shouts and whistles of sheer joy and thanksgiving. Suddenly, rifle shots being fired into the air as part of the celebration echoed across the compound. He leaped to the opening of the tent and screamed:

"Those shooters had better stop immediately or I'll have them in irons!"

The random shots ceased. Unrestrained cries of joy filled the air. It unleashed a large reservoir of relief. Many thought it would never come for them. Silent prayers of thanksgiving filled their hearts. Emile walked to the field kitchen and ordered the mess cooks to run the kitchen at capacity for coffee and warm bread.

A familiar voice called to Emile. "Captain, there's a group of German soldiers a short ways down the east slope who are working on a wounded comrade," Sergeant Ordway pointed to the former enemy soldiers.

Emile grabbed a tankard of coffee and as many mugs as he could carry and walked towards the Germans. They were all young troops like the Americans and were wearing torn and tattered uniforms. They all had that famous thousand-mile-stare from seeing too much of war. Emile was touched, the men were just like his own, weary, frightened, hungry, and jubilant that they had survived the crucible of war. Emile felt that they were brothers in the fraternity of war and was surprised at the compassion he had for them at this time when hours before they were trying to kill each other.

He hailed the group kneeling to care for the soldier on a stretcher on the ground. He offered the coffee and some bread to the hungry Germans. One took a mug of coffee and kneeled down to give the wounded soldier a sip of the warm stimulant. It had been months since they had coffee. Emile passed the tankard of coffee and the mugs to a very young sergeant who was on the verge of tears.

"Here, Sergeant, have some coffee and pass it around. There's more at the field kitchen," Emile said, examining the wounds of the soldier on the pallet.

The wounded German was no older than himself and was missing an arm. A massive amount of blood was oozing from the ragged sleeve. He turned towards his own compound and screamed: "Medic, Medic, I want a medic down here immediately. We have a man who's bleeding to death... hurry..."

Two Army medics carrying a stretcher slid down the slope to the wounded German. One was carrying a bottle of blood plasma. Emile knew what he wanted to do and looked around for a rifle with a bayonet. He saw one on the lip of the trench and pointed to it. "Would someone get me that rifle?"

A reluctant German soldier looked at his friends and after a few words were exchanged in German, he picked it up and handed it to Emile. He drove it securely into the ground and fastened the blood plasma bottle to it while the two medics began to cut away the soldier's uniform exposing the shattered stub just below the elbow. They fashioned a tourniquet to the upper arm and bandaged the stub after smothering it with sulfur powder. The older of the medics took the man's pulse and asked for water, coffee, anything for liquid. The man had to replace a lot of lost blood. He had a vial of morphine that could ease the intense pain for the soldier. He held it up in the air for his friends to look at it.

"Do any of you understand English?"

Emile looked around him, and one private raised his hand. "I speak and understand some English, I spent a summer in England."

"What's your name, soldier?" Emile asked.

"They call me Joseph," the soldier answered.

Joseph," the senior medic explained as he pointed to the morphine, "this medicine is morphine it can give your friend some relief from pain. We'll transport him to our battalion dressing station in a few minutes, but the painkiller will make him much more comfortable. Do I have your permission to administer some to him?"

Joseph spoke a few words to the men around them. Every one of them replied positively, "Ja, ja...."

"Go ahead, medic," Emile said, turning to the large number of German soldiers around them. "We'll take your wounded friend to our hospital where he will be taken care of. Let us put this war behind us and be thankful that we've survived. All of you men are invited to follow me to the field kitchen where we have coffee, bread and fresh ham to eat. You're invited to share our food with us. All of us are a part of the universal band of warriors who suffer the burdens of conducting wars of our nations. Now we are at peace, and you will be safe and welcome to the food and drink available."

Joseph became the spokesman for the German squad who eagerly climbed the slope to the kitchen that was emitting tantalizing aromas of brewed coffee and fresh baked bread. It was a luxury to any infantryman regardless of nationality.

That night, Emile wrote a letter to his wife, telling her about the armistice and the German soldiers who shared food from their field kitchen. The Germans were not supplied as well as the allied troops. All of the participants, Germans as well as British or American soldiers, celebrated the fact that they had survived the holocaust. Later in the day a German officer joined the group about the kitchen. He was enjoying a cup of hot coffee when Emile joined them, selecting a mug of coffee on the serving table.

The German officer spoke to Emile in broken English. "Joseph told me how you took care of one of my men. I want to thank you for that courtesy."

"You're welcome, Major. Word just arrived that he's doing just fine at one of our field hospitals. He's already gone through surgery to stop the bleeding on his arm. Later, he'll get an artificial arm and should be able to function well in society. It was our pleasure to help an injured man in need of treatment. Thank God the guns are silent," Emile explained to the German major.

"Yes, the silence is welcome by all parties," the major acknowledged with a sad, defeated air. "If we could expend as much effort in peacefully settling disagreements as we have in fighting wars the world would be better off, but, alas, that is not the case. I fear that my country is on the verge of anarchy."

"I hope you're wrong, Major. You and your men are free to use the field kitchen as you want. The mess cooks will have eggs, oatmeal, and more bread for breakfast. You are welcome to join us at that time. Our company was the first to arrive in France. I hope it will be the first to be sent back home now that the war is over. I'm anxious to be with my wife."

"Thank you for your generosity, Captain," the German officer saluted him.

14

Emile returned his salute and returned to his tent. He saw two officers waiting for his return. One was the regimental commander, Colonel George Waters. The second man was Lieutenant Colonel Arvard Olsen, the regimental executive officer, a tall husky Swede with blond hair. "I just noticed you in my tent, gentlemen," Emile greeted the officers offering them a cup of coffee from his thermos bottle.

"Colonel Olsen and I have come to tell you that Washington has informed us that we will reduce ranks across the board, and we'll be able to send your company home as fast as transport can be arranged. We also wanted to let you know that you may retain your present rank if you volunteer to stay with the Army in Germany while we're supervising the peace agreement. Your performance has been exemplary, and the Army is always anxious to retain able leaders of men."

Emile knew that the two men meant well and that they were offering him a career in the Army. He was not prepared to make that decision now. He had a powerful need to return home to settle family affairs. "I joined the Maine National Guard and was sent to France when it was activated for duty here. It is my wish to be returned to the states for personal reasons. If that means I have to accept a demotion, so be it, gentlemen. I've heard about the regiment being sent to Russia to guard the Trans Siberian Railroad for the White Russians, and I am not interested in serving there either. Of course, if I'm ordered to do so, I will do my duty, but I will not volunteer at this time."

"Well, Captain, I can't say that I blame you," remarked Colonel Waters. "New orders detaching your company from the Second Division will be issued soon. We're not sure about shipping yet, but you'll be informed as soon as we have transport available to take you to Cherbourg. It's been a pleasure to serve with you and your company from Maine, Captain Ranta."

That next morning, an orderly rider on a motorcycle delivered the orders for their dispatch to the coast. Shortly after, a long line of four-wheel-drive Nash trucks lined up beside the field kitchen to transport them to Cherbourg where a troop transport was waiting to be loaded. They were to leave their tents and all other equipment except personal weapons and supplies which would accompany them onboard the ship readied for their transportation to the New York.

Emile checked each truck as it was loaded, and when everyone in the company was accounted for, he took a seat beside the driver of the first truck. They then began their first steps from the active front towards home. He ordered the convoy to halt at the military cemetery where most of their dead had been buried. Emile climbed down from the truck and ordered the company to form a line beside the cemetery to fire a salute to their fallen brothers. They would remain buried in the soil of France, while they, the living, were going home. It was a solemn moment that evoked deep feelings for all of them. Some felt guilty that they had survived the holocaust of battle.

Emile walked among the rows of white crosses and Stars of David until he came to a marker that read "Sgt. Omar Ranta, 2nd Div., USA." A deep cry of despair pierced his lips as he kneeled beside the grave of his younger brother and traced the etchings in the granite with his soiled fingers. "It really hurts to leave you here alone, Omar. I'm not sure if I'll ever come back to visit your grave. It's important for me to tell you that you'll forever be a part of my life. Ma is gone and is probably with you in the vast world beyond. Take care of her and know that my love is with you both. I wish that it had been me that was taken. You were so young and had much to look forward to, but fate has dealt both of us a different hand to play.

"How proud I am of my younger brother. Your heroism on the battlefield has been an inspiration to all of us who witnessed it. I'll try to be worthy of your sacrifice, Omar. God, I'll miss you and Ma, too. Good-bye…"

Tears fell on the fresh soil of the grave. Emile stood and saluted the granite cross. A cry of longing echoed across the cemetery. Blinded by tears, Emile climbed into the truck telling the driver to proceed. He wiped the tears that ran down his face and stared at the passing landscape, feeling guilty that he was leaving his brother alone in a foreign country. It was difficult to say good-bye.

Several hours later, the ponderous convoy of trucks pulled to a stop beside a large luxury liner on the docks of Cherbourg.

Their Maine National Guard company was the last unit to board the massive ship. Every passageway and room on the ship had been filled to capacity with cots for the troops. They came aboard the ship about the same time as they received several satchels of mail. By the time the liner pulled anchor and entered the English Channel, the mail had been sorted and delivered to the appropriate units scattered throughout the vessel.

Emile received three letters from his wife, Bonnie. They were all dated after the death of his mother. He smiled reading the first two letters with the news and gossip from his small town of Monson on the northern edge of the great Maine woods. It was heavily populated by first and second generations of Swedes and Finns who came to work in the slate quarries scattered throughout the small town.

The third letter was only one page and it hit him with a message that made him ill. He leaned over the rail and emptied his stomach into the churning English Channel. Embarrassed that his friends witnessed the act, he held onto the rail for support and read the letter again:

Dear Emile,

This letter will hurt you and I am powerless to ease the pain. I've put off sharing something with you until I was sure. Today I went to Dr. Varney and he confirmed that I'm pregnant with a child from an old friend of yours, Robert Nasser. It was months ago when he came home on a short leave. I went to see him and things got out of control. To make a long story short, I'm pregnant with his child.

As you know, Robert was killed in France.

May God forgive me for throwing this bomb at you, my faithful husband of two years. I considered killing myself to keep this sordid affair from wreaking havoc with you. I would have except that my mother learned about the situation from the doctor who is a good friend of the family.

Where do we go from here? I ask your forgiveness for my sins and will do anything to salvage our marriage from the scrap heap of despair. I beg you to forgive me, Emile.

If you cannot do that I'll understand…

Bonnie

Two soldiers beside Emile heard him scream and saw him grasp the railing for support. He ripped the letter to shreds, throwing it into the dark waters of the English Channel and collapsed on the deck.

Chapter Three

Five Years Later, April, 1923

Emile was sitting on the beach building a large sand castle with his five-year-old daughter, Faye. She was busy carrying small pails of water to mix with the sand to make it stay together. She was a happy child with long blond hair done up in two braids with a red ribbon tied on the ends, and was enjoying a day at the beach with her daddy. He had promised to help her build the sand castle the next weekend he had off from his duties as a soldier at the Presidio, one of the most beautiful military bases in the country. They had selected a place on the beach at the limit of normal high tides so that they would have a few hours to construct the castle. They had been working diligently on it for a couple of hours. One of the turrets was almost as tall as Faye. She was excited with the way it was turning out. It looked a lot like a real castle in some of her story books.

The tide was coming in, getting closer and closer to the structure. Faye was becoming a little apprehensive that it was going to engulf the castle before she and her father could finish it. "Daddy, the waves are getting closer. I don't want the water to cover my castle."

He looked at her and smiled. "Well, honey, it'll knock the castle down. We knew that would happen when we started it."

It was a battle against time. The first two or three waves slowly crept into the ramparts of the sand castle, undermining the turret and collapsing it. Faye began to cry when the turret fell victim to the oncoming tide.

Emile took her in his strong arms and consoled her. "Don't be sad, honey. The tide has washed it away and carried some of it back out to sea where it will eventually be placed on a beach across the ocean. Perhaps there's a little boy or a little girl across the sea that wants to build a castle like we did, and some of the same sand might be used in their castle. That would be fun to think about, wouldn't it?"

She thought about what her father had told her and felt better about the total destruction of her castle. "Will that little boy or girl build one as big as mine?" she asked innocently with her arm around his neck.

"Probably, Faye. The fun is in the building of the castle, not in having it. You'll always be able to remember how it looked. We should have brought a camera with us, but I didn't think of one."

She looked into his eyes as if she understood what he was saying. Faye's affection for her father was limitless. She loved his easy-going nature and his ability to project an air of security that made her feel good. They were buddies, and whatever her daddy said, she believed. "Is Mommy going to have the baby in the hospital, Daddy?"

"Yes, when it's time, we'll take her to the base hospital. Just think, you'll have a little baby brother or sister to play with. Mommy will be tired when she comes home with the new baby, and you'll be able to help her a lot. I want you to promise to be a good helper when I'm away."

"Why do you have to go away so often, Daddy?"

"I'm a soldier, Faye. When you get older you'll understand," he explained, standing up. The sand castle was completely wiped out as if it had never been there. "Now that the castle is gone, we should go back home to check on Mommy. She often gets tired now. It won't be long before we make that trip to the hospital."

He placed Faye in the front seat of their 1923 Hupmobile touring car and wrapped her up in a blanket. Her bathing suit was soaking wet and she was cold. Her teeth were chattering. They had a few miles to go before they reached their officer's quarters at the base. Faye snuggled in the blanket and leaned against her father. He looked at her and remembered how he had been so angry when he first heard about Bonnie's pregnancy and the child that was not his. It had been a terrible time in his life, almost pushing him to the brink of insanity. Ugly images of Bonnie and another man together were unthinkable. He was determined to divorce her as soon as possible. It was the only option available for him. The anger had no outlet, and he suffered in silence.

Over and over again he asked himself how it could be when he was away in combat. No explanation could possibly make him accept that fact or ease his pain. He came home to Monson late in December, and moved in with his father for the duration of his month's furlough. Everyone in town knew about Bonnie's pregnancy. It was impossible to keep that kind of information quiet in a small New England town. The town was blanketed with several feet of snow when he stepped from the narrow gauge train that was primarily used to transport slate from the quarries that dotted the landscape in Monson. He was the first soldier from Monson to return after the Armistice had been signed.

It had been awkward to talk to folks in the small town, and he was anxious for his furlough to end so that he could get away from the area. He was scheduled to report to Fort Devens in Massachusetts. His father had told him that Bonnie had been ill most of the time he was on furlough. He had refused to see her and had made up his mind to seek a lawyer to get a divorce when he was back at an Army base.

A few days before his furlough was up, Bonnie had showed up at his father's place on the Blanchard Road on the southern shore of Lake Hebron. He had just finished splitting some wood in the shed attached to the house and was washing up at the slate sink in the kitchen when Bonnie walked through the door and carefully closed it behind her. She was dressed in a heavy overcoat with a hood. For a moment neither spoke. It was cold outside, and she carefully unbuttoned the overcoat, removing the hood, letting her long blond hair fall about her shoulders. She was a beautiful girl with blue eyes to match her blond hair and a baby-like complexion. Her Finnish heritage was also evident in her petite physique.

For an instant he had the urge to take her in his arms and hold her. She moved closer to the stove to warm her hands. She was the first to speak. "I know that you hate me now, Emile. I

21

hate the condition that I'm in, too. I just had to see you... We need to talk, Em... my God, I need you to understand..."

"Understand!" he screamed at the top of his lungs. "What is there to understand? Do you have any idea what your action did to me when I was on the other side of the world? Trust and respect have been destroyed by your filthy act. How can I ever be certain it won't happen again? I want out, and I want a divorce as soon as I get to my next duty station next week."

"Would you believe me if I told you that Robert forced me?"

"Not on your life. I knew Bob, and he would not have forced himself on anyone. He's dead now and can't defend himself. That makes it convenient to blame him."

She began to cry and took a seat in a chair next to the stove. "It's true, Em. I never led him on. I swear, I never did... You've got to believe me..."

He felt helpless. He wanted to believe her, but she was carrying another man's child. Forgiving and forgetting were two different virtues. "I loved you with all my heart. When it was difficult in the trenches of France, all I had to do was thank God for you and it was easier to take. Now, that's all gone. I'm confused and angry. The picture of you with another man is driving me crazy."

Bonnie blew her nose in a handkerchief and got up to leave. "I've contacted a retired doctor in Guilford who will do an abortion. Will that make any difference with you, Em? Don't continue to avoid me as if I never existed. I need to hear it from you. Do you want me to have an abortion? My mother and father are sick about my decision. At this time in my crisis, I'm begging you to help me... Oh God, I need you, Em..."

He had been considering what she had told him, and the idea that the baby would not be a problem appealed to him. It would eliminate a lot of talk around town. Suddenly, it struck him that he was selfishly thinking of himself. He knew that she was at a dangerous stage of desperation and was about to take a step that could end the baby's life and her own. That truly frightened him. If what she had told him was true, then he was being selfish, and she was bearing the trauma of her condition alone. His abandonment of her since he received that hateful letter that announced her condition suddenly made him ashamed of his actions. He should have given her an opportunity to explain what happened, and asked himself if he was man enough to give her another chance.

"I don't want you to go to a quack doctor and risk that something could go wrong," he exclaimed, reaching for her. "I've been selfish. The baby you're carrying is unable to defend its right to live. If you're willing, I'm willing, Bonnie. The thought that I might lose you forever is frightening to me." He would have to control those ugly images that hurt. Just possibly, losing Bonnie forever would hurt even more. It was an important decision he had to make.

He could still recall that magic moment. She had lifted her lips to him and uttered a sigh, "God has answered my prayers."

From that day on, the two of them never discussed the genesis of the baby that was about to be an important part of their lives. Emile's decision to stay in the Army meant that he had to take a cut in rank and pay to that of a first lieutenant. He had checked the possibility of work and was shocked at the scarcity of jobs available in the private sector. He had discussed that situation with Bonnie in his father's kitchen that day, and she cried for a long time holding her head in her two hands. This time they were tears of thanksgiving and joy. How comforting it was to hold her close to him. Their love for each other had been severely tested. It was a happy couple that left Monson together on the train to Brownville Junction where they took a Boston and Maine train directly to Fort Devens in northern Massachusetts.

Their stay at Fort Devens was brief. Rapid changes were taking place in the Army. The war in France had made it possible for the U.S. Army to evolve from an efficient constabulary force to that of an army capable of organizing and managing large formations of men in combat. Emile was ordered to what was to become the Army's premier infantry school at Fort Benning, a few miles south of Columbus, Georgia. The Army was finally entering the 20th century and was laying the foundation for what was to become the finest fighting formation in the world. Desperately needed changes were underway if the country was to take its place among the major players in the world.

They traveled by train to Columbus where they rented a small house a few miles from the camp. There was no hospital on the base, only a small infirmary for minor injuries and ailments. He was a part of the first class at Benning and was disappointed at the primitiveness of the base. There were no permanent buildings or facilities for training or housing the troops, so they started in tents and had to build their log cabin huts from scratch. Emile had to stay on base during the week and was able to spend the weekends with Bonnie.

What they lacked in physical facilities, they made up for in quality of instruction. The base would in the future become famous for its high standards and quality of instruction. It was attended regularly by Army officers, Marine Corps officers, and soldiers from friendly nations. The classes were separated into two groups: those that covered the management of battalions, regiments, and regimental combat teams in every imaginable situation fertile minds could conjure up; and those that covered commands of divisions and brigades. Higher commands of corps and army groups were a part of the education of higher ranks at Leavenworth and the Army schools at Carlisle Barracks in Pennsylvania.

During this formation period, Bonnie was physically getting more and more uncomfortable. The summer heat and humidity in central Georgia was uncomfortable for everybody. There were several officers' families living near them in Columbus who were a great help to Bonnie during her pregnancy. The wives formed a valuable support system for soldiers' families making it possible for the student soldiers to apply all of their energy to their training without needless distraction on the home front. Bonnie was quick to appreciate the unselfish aid and care provided by the women who were a large part of the life of a career soldier. Their efforts made life in the military more enjoyable. The fraternity of the members was sincere. The wives' telegraph was perhaps the most efficient intelligence system in the Army, capable of predicting, with astonishing accuracy, events on the post. It was a secure group that linked their collective arms around those most in need of support.

Emile and Bonnie had joined a small unique slice of Americana whose lives were highly regimented and structured in the Army tradition of the period.

Chapter Four

Emile and Faye had collected their things at the beach after the tide had worn away all evidence of the sand castle. They headed home to officer's quarters at the Presidio anxious to check on Bonnie. He had made an appointment to take her to the base doctor. She was close to the time for her delivery.

When they arrived home they found Bonnie sitting on a couch in the living room with her bag packed beside her, waiting impatiently for them to return. She had felt pains all morning and knew it would not be long. Her water had burst, and she had to change into a clean set of clothes.

Emile saw the desperate look on her face and knew. "How far apart are the pains, Bonnie?"

"About ten minutes, Em. We better go to the hospital. My water has broken, and I'm awfully uncomfortable," she cried, reaching for him.

"Of course you are," he replied, helping her to the door. "Faye, would you drag your mother's bag to me on the porch? We've got to get to the hospital as soon as possible," he ordered. He was worried. Bonnie did not look good, and she was crying. He should have cut his time on the beach shorter.

Faye had been a silent witness to what was taking place and was frightened. Emile leaned down to hug her and placed her in the back seat of the automobile. "Don't let all of this emotion frighten you, Faye. Soon everything will be fine."

Within a few minutes they arrived at the hospital, where two attendants offered to take her into the facility. Emile placed Bonnie's bag on the portable stretcher, and she was taken into the maternity delivery room. The nurse told Emile that it might be a long wait. No one can predict. He took that opportunity to take Faye to a neighbor who had agreed to care for her while her mother was in the hospital.

"Now, be a good girl, and Daddy will pick you up as soon as the new baby arrives," he told her, anxious to return to the hospital.

"I will, Daddy. Mommy was crying a lot, and I was scared for her," she stammered not happy being left alone.

"That's normal, honey. Mommy will be just fine. She's in good hands right now, and we have got to be patient. The new baby girl or boy will not come into this world until ready." He gave Faye a reassuring hug and rushed to the Hupmobile.

On the way back to the hospital, he thought about suitable names for the new life that would become their responsibility. He and Bonnie had spoken about it often, but came up with nothing definite. If it was a boy, he had entertained the name "Alpha". It is from the first letter of the Greek alphabet, denoting a beginning. He had met a fine Marine infantry officer in the war named Alpha Bower. They had become good friends and kept in touch with each other after the war. Alpha was living in Hawaii.

Bonnie's delivery was prolonged into the next day. Emile was getting exhausted and drank cup after cup of coffee, waiting for his son or daughter to be born. He had time to renew events in his life since returning home from France. He knocked the ashes from his pipe and leaned back in the comfortable chair of the waiting room to relax. The room was empty, and he closed his eyes thinking of those parts of his life that were still fresh in his memory.

The first child that Bonnie brought into the world was Faye, a love child with an old friend and classmate as her father. He loved her without exceptions and had always been proud to call her his daughter. He honestly believed that she deserved that kind of love. However, there was a time when her presence only reminded him that he was not her father and another man had satisfied his pleasure with his wife.

He and Bonnie had agreed beforehand that if she had a girl it would be named after Bonnie's mother, Faye. All during the pregnancy, Emile constantly assured his wife that he was ready to accept the truth and vowed never to mention the circumstances of her condition again. He had honored that vow. The past was history and could never be changed. They optimistically looked forward to the future.

The evening a nurse came into the waiting room of the hospital in Columbus, Georgia, to announce that he was the father of a healthy baby girl, he was relieved that Bonnie had come through the ordeal well. His first view of Faye in the maternity ward had evoked a wrenching sickness that he could not control. Images of his wife with another man instantly filled his head when he first saw Faye in her arms being breast-fed. In that moment he viewed Faye as a threat to their marriage and to his peace of mind. He doubted if he could play the role of a doting father as he had so faithfully promised.

Bonnie saw the mixed emotions on his face. "Isn't she a beautiful child, Em? Don't let your imagination run wild... Little Faye had no choice in selecting her parents. She's ours now and cannot defend herself against those thoughts running through your head." Bonnie began to cry. "She needs both of us. There's no one else to care for her. Please, I was hoping her birth would unite us more than ever. The look on your face is frightening, and it will tear you apart if you can't accept this beautiful little girl..."

He had listened to his wife's plea for acceptance. The things she had said were all true... but he was having trouble controlling his emotions, and was fully aware of the fact that environment influenced the growth and development of a child more than their genetic makeup. He hunched his shoulders and looked at Bonnie. "I'm glad that you've come through fine giving birth to little Faye, the new member of our family. Your mother will be happy to be a grandmother, especially when they share the same name. Give me time, Bonnie," he said, bending over to kiss her.

Just then, little Faye reached out to touch his chin. The soft touch electrified him. He took her tiny hand in his and marveled over the perfect fingers and nails already grown. It was like a bolt of lightning had struck him. It was a pivotal moment in his life that he could still recall with clarity and heavy emotions. His daughter was telling him, in the only way possible, that she needed him to protect and look after her. Tears welled in his eyes when she clasped her fingers about his thumb. In that moment, she had won the heart of her daddy the way little girls have done since time began.

Emile could still recall that spiritual moment in his life with a warm glow of pride that he was able to erase the bad dreams from his mind. After that moment of discovery, he never questioned what Bonnie had told him. He loved her very much. She and Faye gave meaning to his life. Bonnie had made their home a refuge from the outside pressures by being her natural generous self. He was always proud to show her off to his brother officers. She had fit in well to that select group of couples who made up the heart and soul of the Army. They were often isolated from mainstream life, yet they remained the nucleus that defined the Army at that time. Duty, honor, country, were the code in which soldiers and their families lived and worked. Their loyalty and devotion to the country and to each other was often taken for granted, especially in times of peace.

Emile was hopeful to be assigned to his old company, but openings were not available. He was assigned as an executive officer to a company that was a part of his original regiment. Most of the officers were different from the ones he had served with in France. In the peacetime Army he could expect to take ten years to make captain again. Advancements were slow, and many good men lost interest and resigned their commissions for more lucrative civilian jobs. He had written to several companies who hired foresters. Every answer to his query was the same polite "no". That was when he decided to stay in the Army. He had always enjoyed the camaraderie that existed in the regulated environment. Once he accepted the decision, he was well aware that it was a difficult life for wives who had to endure and adapt to the needs of the Army, which were often severe and unfair.

Emile's journey down memory lane was interrupted by a nurse. "Lieutenant Ranta, your wife is resting easy. You have a healthy baby boy. Congratulations!"

The words, 'baby boy' got his attention. "Thank you, nurse. It's been a long night, but the news that we have a son has made it all worthwhile."

"Your wife is taking a well-earned rest right now while we take care of the baby. Why don't you go back to quarters and get some rest, too? Your new baby boy will need all of your attention later on. I'm happy for you."

"That's sound advice, nurse. I am tired. Our little girl will be thrilled with the news that she has a baby brother." Emile left the hospital to pick up Faye at the neighbor's apartment.

While he was at the apartment, he learned that the company had received verbal orders to prepare for expeditionary duty in South America. Portions of the regiment had already been shipped to Louisiana and Florida. Emile was executive officer of his company and drove hurriedly with Faye to the post command center to find out just what was going on. He had a bad feeling that he was going to leave Bonnie and Faye with the new baby, Alpha, to care for alone. It was typical of what the Army expected of its soldiers. The company commander, Captain Mitch O'Connor, was at the center and told him it meant duty in Haiti. He told him about the new baby and Bonnie.

"Congratulations, Emile," Captain O'Connor told him. "This notice of a move to Haiti is sudden to say the least. The Marines are unable to respond in regimental configuration just now. Law and order in Haiti is lost, and the country is in desperate need of food, medicine supplies, and martial law. That's all I can tell you, Emile."

He left the center and went to the company command post where he ordered an officer conference in an hour. Then he and Faye raced to the hospital to visit with Bonnie and Alpha. Emile quickly described the emergency situation to Bonnie, concluding that she might be able to get some help from her parents while he was away for an extended period of time.

"Emile," she cried with alarm in her eyes. "What am I to do?" she asked helplessly.

"I'm really sorry, Bonnie. I'm a soldier, and we discussed these types of scenarios before we jointly made the decision to stay in the Army. I'm sure that every family left on the base will be able and willing to assist you in many ways. It's part of an old Army custom. We look after each other and that includes families. Please, Bonnie, I'm not to blame for these types of emergencies. I'm just as concerned as you are, trust me, honey. I'd ask for a release from the company, but I'm the exec officer and can't quit without damaging my career."

"You could resign from the Army, Emile..."

That statement surprised him. "You don't mean that, Bonnie. Resigning in the middle of a crisis could land me in jail or dismissal from the Army for cowardice attached to my permanent record. No, you can't really want me to quit just because it's going to be tough for a few days."

Bonnie saw the impossible situation she was demanding of him and changed the discussion, asking him to raise the hospital bed so that the nurse could bring Alpha to her. "Would you like to hold your new brother, Faye?"

It was a distraction from the heavy conversation that could go on forever. "Faye has been worried about her mom, and is looking forward to helping, aren't you, Faye?"

"Daddy made me promise to help, and I will, Mommy," she exclaimed, as the nurse entered the room with the new baby. She looked at him as the nurse gently placed him in her mother's arms. "Was I that small?"

"Listen, Bonnie," Emile bent down to kiss her and Alpha on the cheek. "I've called for an officers' conference and will leave Faye here with you for a while. Hopefully, I'll have more specific information when I stop by to pick up Faye. Be patient, Bonnie. I'm doing the best I can."

"I know that, Em, it just came at such a bad time for the family. I understand that you must do your duty. Go, and don't worry about us."

Emile hugged them both and returned to the command post where everybody was busy getting ready to deploy. Specific orders were issued instructing the regiment to proceed to northern Haiti and land at a location capable of unloading their transport. They were to proceed to Cap Haitien, the second largest city in Haiti where they were to restore order in conjunction with the existing government.

Things were happening fast. Emile would not be able to wait until Bonnie was discharged from the hospital. He knew it was going to be difficult for her to handle the days ahead, but orders were orders, and they had to be obeyed. His company was ordered to draw equipment and supplies for thirty days in the field. Transport to the southern tip of the Florida Keys was to be done by rail where ships would be waiting to take them to Haiti.

Emile had intensely trained the company to the point where they were looking forward to field duty to get away from training exercises. He was notified that the company commander had broken his leg that evening. The regiment offered the command to Emile with a brevet rate of Captain for the duration of their tour of duty in Haiti.

For the next twenty-four hours, Emile was a busy man, drawing equipment and supplies for the company and establishing an understanding with several wives to step in to help Bonnie if she needed it. He was gratified that the women took it as an honor to look after their own. They asked Emile to do his duty without a worry that his wife and family would be looked after. It was that old Army fraternity of brotherhood that worked like a charm when needed.

Emile spent the last two hours with Bonnie before he had to turn out the company for transport to the local railroad station. Bonnie was not happy with the situation and let him know how difficult it would be for her.

"Listen, Bonnie," he exclaimed impatiently, "I've done everything I could to arrange help for you and the children. I realize it's a bad situation for you, but almost every family on the post is going through the same hardships. You know better than me how well the wives support each other."

"I know that, Emile. It's just that I had planned our lives around our new son and was looking forward to being a family again. The Army seems to have priority on your time…"

"Bonnie, nothing has changed since you and I had that long conversation about my remaining in the Army. Don't you remember? The Army is doing what the country asks it to do, and we have to comply, regardless of the hardships."

Bonnie was exhausted from the delivery and laid her head back on the pillow. "I'm sorry for acting this way, Em. I know that what you are saying is true, but..."

Emile placed a finger to her lips and said: "I understand, Bonnie. I have to run. I'll be in touch as often as possible. You and the kids will always be in my thoughts. Good-bye my love."

Emile quickly exited the ward and rushed to an officer conference. He was late. His first sergeant met him at the command post door to confirm his promotion to a Brevet Captain with full responsibility for the company.

Chapter Five

The infantry elements of the regiment left the Presidio on a Union Pacific train a few hours after Emile said good-bye to Bonnie and the children. Its motorized vehicles and other equipment were being shipped via a separate rail line. Their destination was the Florida Keys where the Navy was waiting for them. Emile knew all of the platoon leaders in his company and delegated a lot of the responsibility for the equipment and personal outfitting of the men to those lieutenants.

He busied himself to studying all the information he could get on Haiti and its people. His knowledge of French would be helpful. Haiti was a troubled country with a chronic history of revolution after revolution to install governments that represented the strongest body of thugs and parasites who fed off the poor people until a different element was installed. Some administrations lasted only hours, others were lucky to survive a year.

Haiti is a very poor country and has remained that for the past century and a half since the French settled the colony. It is a country of about two million people with most of them speaking French. The black population is mostly illiterate and is dominated by a small percentage of Franco-black mulattos who have grown rich off government jobs, contracts, and good old fashioned graft. The two classes hate each other, and the elites run the country. The national treasury is always empty because it is used to continue the fight against opposing forces and to keep the current regime in power.

The trip to Haiti gave Emile a chance to review his life and the decisions he had made that were seriously affecting his family. Bonnie was not happy with his unexpected posting to North America. His absence made it necessary for her to take over the running of the household alone immediately after childbirth. It was inherently unfair, but there was nothing he could do about it. This time, she made him regret the decision to stay in the Army. Jobs were scarce, and the Army provided the funds necessary to survive as a family. There was no other alternative available to him, and out of desperation he made the choice for the family and signed on.

Officer conferences on the trip were designed to provide a background for their mission in Haiti. The French and Americans controlled the National Bank with a fortune in gold bullion stored in its vaults. They had been attacked frequently by the "Cacos", one of the largest bands of revolutionaries in the impoverished country. Their name comes from a native bird that has a call kao-coo, kao-coo! The bandits grew rich off government contracts, and graft. Most were illiterate and poor. They hated the small number of French-speaking black mulattos who dominated the national and local government positions.

The country of Haiti was in shambles. Any improvements made by friendly powers, primarily the United States or France, were soon destroyed when the regime in power was opposed. There was a continuous battle for supremacy. Few governments lasted more than a few months. The government in power lived well off the national treasury. If the current government ceased to pay the bandits, then another revolution took place to change the government. It was an endless cycle of violence, theft, corruption, and destruction. Presidents were often changed on a monthly basis. One of the missions of the American Army intervention was to remove the gold bullion from the bank vaults and transport it to a Navy gunship for safe keeping.

The evening before the soldiers were to land at Cap-Haitien Emile sat in his bunk and wrote a letter to Bonnie:

Somewhere in the Caribbean

My Dearest Wife,

Tonight my thoughts are with you and the children. I miss you a lot and am sorry that I had to leave you alone at such an important time. My choice of a career has caused you more distress than I expected. Our new baby boy will enrich our lives and I pray that you are getting the help you need from the other wives at the post. The wives of Army personnel are an integral part of the team, and they keep the home fires burning smoothly. Don't hesitate to ask them for help.

I can't tell you where I'm going. I suspect that the newspapers will be reporting on our expedition and you'll know more about it than we do. It appears to be more of a humanitarian mission than anything else. Rest assured that I'll take good care of myself, so don't worry about your husband who loves you very much. Give my love to Faye and little Alpha.

My family is always in my thoughts, goodnight my love.

Emile

The large transport arrived in the West Indies and dropped anchor in a harbor on the north shore of the island of Hispaniola which is shared by Haiti and the Dominican Republic. The main mission for the regiment was to proceed to Cap-Haitien, the second largest city in Haiti, on the north shore. There they were ordered to relieve the French troops that were defending the National Bank, built by the French one hundred years ago. Once that had been accomplished, the Americans were ordered to remove the gold bullion in its vaults, and transport it to the Navy gunships that had accompanied them to the West Indies.

The United States had received hegemony for the region ever since the end of the Spanish American War. Endemic strife and conflict was normal. Maintaining the peace was almost impossible. Any improvements made by earlier efforts of American soldiers and marines were soon destroyed during one of the revolutions. Emile was the first soldier to land on the island. He directed the landing of supplies and equipment necessary for the troops to conduct their mission.

Horses were the first ashore. Emile and most of his officers were mounted on horseback. Wheeled vehicles were at times more trouble than they were worth in the rugged terrain they would encounter to and from the National Bank, so he decided to march the column to and from the bank. They were directed to maintain the peace in and around the bank while the bullion was being loaded on the Army wagons, and to protect the diplomats at the International compound near the bank. The column spread out along a road that was not much more than a cart track with Emile leading the way. He had dispatched flank patrols and scouts to check ahead of the column. Bandits were numerous in the vicinities of the roadways. People passed at their risk.

Crumbling buildings were found along the way, giving the impression that they were empty, but Emile had been warned that they were generally inhabited by the infamous Cacos bandits. They arrived at the center of Cap-Haitien by mid-day. The streets were littered with ruble and appeared empty, but an experienced eye could detect wary onlookers behind the ruble checking to see if the column was friend or foe. When Emile ordered the American flag unfurled, more people appeared to greet them as saviors. Hunger was rampant in the city, and many held out their hands for food. Emile had anticipated such an incident and had carried extra food in the wagons. He ordered it to be dispensed to those who asked for food and warned them against trickery of any kind. The column was not to stop. He repeated that statement several times reminding the men of their primary mission.

They were met at the bank by relieved French officials and soldiers with Mauser rifles. Emile saluted the officials and dismounted to hand them the official request to transfer the gold bullion to the United States for safekeeping. He also immediately established a number of guards to surround the area while the transfer was taking place. He had several machine guns mounted on horse-drawn carriages. The French officials were pleased to see that the column was a formidable force.

A French official read the orders in silence and said in broken English, "I'm from the French detachment and have been authorized to make the transfer for safekeeping while we settle the revolution. I see that you are well prepared to defend your column, Captain."

"Yes, Sir," Emile replied. "An American gunboat is standing off your northern coast ready to receive the gold. It will be well protected, Sir. I have a whole regiment to defend the column. We should not have any trouble safely delivering the bullion to the U.S. Navy."

"We are thankful for that, Captain, but be alert for trouble from the large number of Cacos in the area. They'll take any risk to seize the bullion. Whoever has the gold controls the government. Chaos exists all through the country. Peace and tranquility are rare commodities," the official said as he shook his head in despair.

"By the way, how much gold bullion is involved?"

The official pointed to the column of wagons that rode in the center of the column: "Three wagons will be sufficient for the transfer, Captain. The current government is in the process of being evicted from power. Just how long that will be is unknown."

Emile was amazed. Three wagons full of gold was a fortune beyond his ability to comprehend. He stood by the entrance of the bank while the transfer was taking place and alerted those within his voice range to be vigilant for any sign of opposition. He ordered the men to lock and load their rifles and be ready for instant response to trouble.

When the wagons were filled, Emile said good-bye to the French officials and immediately ordered the column to advance to the coast with every man on the alert for trouble. It took several hours for the column to reach the coast where they were met by a contingent of armed sailors who were authorized to take control of the transfer from the wagons to the small motor boats that would carry it to the cruiser anchored just off shore. The cruiser's big guns stood ready to secure the perimeter of the area if trouble erupted. Emile was relieved to hand over the responsibility to the Navy.

Once the gold had been safely secured in the holds of the cruiser, Emile received new orders to conduct a patrol of battalion size to secure a major bridge on a road that led from the coast to Cap Haitien. Rebel forces had seized the bridge and were demanding outrageous tolls from anyone passing over it. Emile volunteered to lead the battalion on the patrol when he heard that the commander of the battalion had injured his leg falling from the upper deck on the cruiser.

The battalion landed at a small inlet to reach the roadway. The jungle was so thick it was almost impossible to penetrate. The bridge was about three miles inland from the coast. The so-called roadway was nothing more than a rough cart track that had been hacked from the jungle. He knew that if he stayed on the road without flank protection that he was inviting trouble. Therefore, he asked some of the men from his original Maine National Guard unit to volunteer for that mission. It was a difficult task in the thick jungle, but several volunteered to patrol about fifty feet to each side of the road.

The battalion proceeded slowly on foot for about an hour when the sharp crack of a Krag rifle erupted on the left flank. Emile was at the point of the column and instantly ordered the men to seek cover. Gunfire came from both sides of the road. The captain of one of the companies fell to the road unable to crawl to some cover. Emile saw the man go down and rushed to assist him when he felt a sharp burning sensation in his abdomen. It spun him around and he fell in the center of the road where his blood mixed with the mud in the track.

Chapter Six

The gentle rocking motion of the large freighter was the first sensation Emile felt since he was shot and lost consciousness on the jungle-covered roadway in Haiti. He opened his eyes and asked, "Where am I?" in a strained bewildered voice.

A Navy nurse bent over his cot relieved that he was talking. "You've been wounded, Captain. You're on a Navy ship off the coast of Haiti heading for Florida."

"I can't move my arms," Emile hysterically cried. "I can't move my arms..."

"Hush, now, Captain," the nurse whispered in his ear. "We have a number of wounded soldiers that are resting now. Do not be alarmed. Your men wrapped you like a mummy in the jungle and rushed you to the coast where a Navy patrol boat brought you to this ship. They did the best they could to control the bleeding. You have multiple bullet wounds, the most serious being in your stomach. The doctors will remove the wrappings shortly. They have been busy caring for the most seriously wounded men from your patrol. You should try to drink as much as possible. You've lost a lot of blood."

"Cold water will be welcome," he responded.

He was relieved and grieved to learn what the nurse had told him. "My God, I hope the men don't believe that I led them into a trap. How many were wounded?"

"I don't know how many were killed, Captain. There are eight men from your company on board this ship," the nurse told him.

"I passed out when we were ambushed by a large number of Cacos on the cart track," Emile replied in a wavering voice.

"Rest easy, Captain."

Two days later, Emile was sitting in a wheelchair on the deck of the freighter watching the most beautiful sunset he had ever experienced. The wounds on his stomach and right arm had been cleaned and dressed with bandages. He was lucky; no bones were broken by the bullets that violated his body. He did have a few cracked ribs and had lost his spleen. The doctors had assured him that people can live without a spleen.

The ship had just met with a Navy destroyer that had transported mail for the ship and for the new Army patients on board. It raised the morale of the men several degrees. Letters from home were precious gifts. Emile was no exception. He had two letters from Bonnie, recognizing her distinctive penmanship on the envelopes. He opened the oldest postmarked letter and settled into his chair to read:

June 20, 1923

My Darling Husband;

I'd like to believe that I've grown up and am a little bit wiser than I was on the day that you left to do your duty. My reaction to your leaving was selfish and immature, and I'm writing to ask for your forgiveness.

You had told me about support from soldiers' wives, and I can tell you that it is so true. They all made my transition from the hospital to our quarters so easy. I've become close friends with several of them. I better understand now what you say about the fraternity of brothers that exists among Army families. Forgive me for sending you away under a black cloud. I promise to make it up to you.

Our new son, Alpha, is doing just fine. I'm nursing him and he's already gained a few pounds. Little Faye has been a wonderful helper. She can change Alpha's diapers now.

I send my love to you by the full moon that shines through the window. May God keep you safe until you return.

All my love,

Bonnie

41

The letter made him feel ten feet tall. He had been apprehensive about leaving, yet he knew that the other wives at the base would react the way Bonnie had described. That night he wrote to tell her about his wounds and that they would heal in time without complications. They would not interfere with his decision to stay in the Army. Lieutenant Harper, a platoon leader in his regiment had also been wounded and was on the ship with Emile. The lieutenant had told him about openings that were available to officers to apply for admittance to the well-respected French Ecole Superieure de Guerre in Paris. It was available for any officer who could read and speak French. Emile was immediately interested. It would be a chance for him and Bonnie to be together for an extended period of time in a part of the world that she would enjoy. He told her that he was going to apply for selection as soon as he was released from the hospital and his wounds had healed.

Thoughts about his performance in Haiti filled his head especially in the evenings when the ward was quiet and the soft hum of the powerful engines on the ship were comforting. The force he had led into the jungle to defend a bridge was, in his mind, a failure. He never made it to the bridge. He learned later that the bridge was eventually blown to bits by the revolutionaries that had ambushed his force. The losses saddened him, and he searched in vain for the chance that if he had done things differently, he could have avoided the casualties. If their sacrifices had helped to make the corrupt country a better place for the people, he could accept it, but no matter what was done in a country like Haiti, nothing would change except for the names of the current leaders.

Emile's ship docked in Florida where a train was available to take him and the other wounded to the Presidio at San Francisco. An hour after he arrived at the base, Bonnie and Faye visited him with his new son, Alpha, wrapped in a blanket. It was a happy scene. Bonnie laid Alpha on the pillow beside Emile's head. Tiny fingers grasped Emile's finger. He kissed it and had marveled at the small nails and dimples on the hand. A warm glow settled over Emile as he kissed the small hand in his.

Bonnie saw the fatigue in Emile's eyes and cut their first visit short so that he could rest after the tiring trip from Florida. She bent over and kissed him. "Thank God you're home with us safe and sound. What do the doctors say about your career in the Army?"

"They have assured me that I'll be back doing full duties in a month or so," he informed her. He then mentioned the prospects for admittance to the French War College and that he was applying for one of the openings as soon as he could.

She seemed pleased at the prospect of a posting in Paris. "That sounds great for all of us, Em. Now you rest and we'll see you tomorrow."

"It's great to be back with my family. I've missed all of you a lot. I'm a lucky soldier."

Emile's condition continued to improve once he arrived at the Presidio. The physical therapy routines were arduous and demanding. He had always believed that he was in good physical condition, but the extreme effort the drills demanded of him indicated that he was softer than he thought. He had applied for the opening available for the French school that week.

One day after he had completed physical therapy exercises and taken a shower, he was surprised to see Colonel George Waters walk into the ward.

"It's nice to see a friendly face, Colonel," Emile explained.

"I stopped by to congratulate you, Emile. You've been approved for the next session of the French War College. It's a rare privilege, and I'm glad to see that you were selected. Sometimes the Army does do things right." He smiled and shook Emile's hand. "I thought you had enough of France when you left after the war."

"Well, Sir, I thought it might be good for me and the family. I've got to brush up on my French though. The Canadian French is quite different from that spoken in Paris. Once I decided to stay in the Army, I was anxious to attend all of the command schools I could get into. They will prepare me for higher commands. I owe the troops in my commands the very best."

"You're ambitious, Emile. I always liked that about you. I wanted to congratulate you and wish you the best. You were a superb officer in our old regiment. I was fortunate to have you aboard."

"Thank you, Sir. I really appreciate your sentiments. I have to be honest, I was glad to get out of Haiti. It's a cesspool of corruption and filth with little chance for improvement."

"I agree with you, Emile. You take care and keep us informed how you like the new posting." Colonel Waters shook his hand and left the room.

A month after Emile left Haiti, he was declared physically fit for command and was discharged from the Presidio Hospital. He had orders to attend the next rotation of soldiers attending the French Ecole Superieure de Guerre (French War College) the first of September, 1923. He rushed to their quarters to share the news with Bonnie. They had discussed the possibility of spending some well-earned leisure time prior to his scheduled courses touring France with the family. They both agreed that it was a good time for them to purchase an automobile for use in France to visit portions of the country. Emile had a friend who was enthusiastic about his newly purchased Hupmobile, so they bought a brand new Hupmobile touring sedan.

A large Army transport ship was being loaded with supplies in the Boston Harbor. The vessel was operated by the Army Quartermaster Corps which had more ships than the Navy. Army personnel and their families were moved to distant posts by the transports at no added costs to the Army. An Army Quartermaster was in charge of the ship.

Bonnie had questioned Emile about that, and he had replied: "In the Navy and the Coast Guard, the man in charge of a ship is called the Captain. In the Merchant Marine he's called a Master. The Army calls him a Quartermaster. They all have different names but share the same responsibilities on the ship."

They had a fairly rough trip across the North Atlantic in the early fall and were safely landed in Cherbourg, France, on the English Channel. Their Hupmobile and all of their luggage were quickly off-loaded by mid-morning. It was a cool, windy day, and they were anxious to drive to Paris before nightfall so that they could get settled into their new apartment near the school.

Emile was given the assignment to the French War College for one year because he was fluent in reading and writing French. His mother was French from Montreal, Canada, and had insisted that he learn English and French while he was growing up. Mastering the language was the secret in doing well at the school where a lot of time was spent learning how to use supporting arms in a variety of different situations.

The French school expanded on the courses he had taken at Fort Benning. French field orders differed from the conventional United States Army orders containing five short paragraphs, leaving the methodology of execution to the officer on the ground. The French, however, also stated how to implement the order, discouraging initiative on the part of the subordinate. The American system was much superior and more efficient in the heat of combat, Emile believed.

He and the family left Paris a year later believing that Benning had given him a more secure feeling in his ability to command a battalion or a regiment. He believed that the U.S. Army was composed of a larger number of self-reliant men more able to think for themselves. The French were less flexible and were often bogged down by traditions of another era. When an American unit lost its commander on the battlefield, it was not uncommon for a sergeant or even a corporal to rally the men to complete their mission. The French did not grant their enlisted men that opportunity. Resourcefulness was a major component in any American unit from the private to the top ranking officer.

While Emile was busy at the school, Bonnie and the children enjoyed the hustle and bustle of the capital city of France. Paris was all that Bonnie had imagined, and occasionally, she had a French woman take care of the children while she attended exciting times at the theatre, at the opera house, and on tourist excursions within the large city.

Emile had spent every working hour studying or attending classes, leaving very little time with the family. The tour of France that they had planned prior to the scheduled course at the school had to be cancelled because his courses started earlier than expected. He and Bonnie often had harsh words with each other about his inattention to her and the children. She had anticipated more time with him.

He became exhausted from the demanding schedule and the anxious discourse that was developing between them. She had repeatedly asked him to skip as many classes as possible. Emile tried to explain how important classes and study periods were to his future in the Army. He was not at liberty to skip school like a teenager in high school. That argument was completely unacceptable to Bonnie. That selfish side of her that he had never known became more dominant than ever for the duration of his stay at the French school.

One year later, Emile was impatiently waiting for Bonnie to return to the apartment. She had gone shopping at the last minute prior to attending the very formal graduation exercises at the college. Faye and Alpha were both dressed for the occasion and were quietly waiting while Emile completed dressing in his best uniform. He checked in the mirror to be certain that his rows of service ribbons were in perfect alignment and that his Sam Browne belt was polished.

"Well, kids," he announced, walking into the living room. "I hope your mother comes soon, I don't want to be late for this solemn occasion."

"Mommie has been shopping a lot lately," remarked Faye.

"Why do you say that, Honey?" Emile asked, looking out the window.

"While you were away at school, we often stayed with the lady next door who told us that Mommie was shopping," Faye replied.

Emile smiled at her. "Well, it isn't every day that your mother has a chance to spend time shopping in Paris. We were lucky to be assigned to this school in such a historical city."

Just then, Bonnie burst through the door with her arms full of packages. "I know that I'm late, and I'm sorry," she exclaimed.

"We should be leaving now, Bonnie," he stated, noting that she was not dressed suitably for a graduation ceremony. Her low-cut dress and her disheveled appearance annoyed him, and he was trying hard to control his patience. "If you hurry, we've got time for you to slip into something more appropriate."

She quickly eyed Faye and Alpha making certain that they were dressed properly, and ran into the bedroom. "I'll only be a minute, Emile. I didn't realize it was so late."

Emile checked his watch and shook his head in disgust. He was angry that she could be so cavalier about the graduation that was the culmination a lot of hard work on his part. He was sick thinking that she did not share his enthusiasm or appreciation for the effort he was making to insure a better future for the family.

The fact that they had failed to cultivate a more intimate and meaningful relationship on this tour saddened him. It seemed that nothing he did satisfied her. Arguments became louder and more inflamed than ever. Quiet moments were no longer filled with peace and security. He was becoming more and more depressed. The tour of duty he had just completed should have been a period of celebration. Instead, it ended in hurt feelings. His Bonnie had changed!

Chapter Seven

The graduation ceremony was conducted with pomp and precision as expected by the prestigious French War College. There were several officers from nations around the world in attendance. One younger American, Captain Carl Webber, was a U.S. Marine who became Emile's best friend during the exacting routines the French had put them through. They had gotten together often when Carl came to their apartment for a meal and a study session.

Their training had prepared them for staff positions where defense policies are crafted and implemented. Emile had already been informed that his next duty station was to be Washington, D.C. Carl had been promoted to a Major and was ordered to the staff of the Commandant of the Marine Corps, also in Washington. They decided to celebrate the day together at a French restaurant on the Champ de Mars near the French College campus.

After the graduation ceremonies, Emile and Carl walked together to meet Bonnie and the children. They had obtained the services of a nanny to take care of Faye and Alpha back at the apartment and drove there to drop them off in their brand new Hupmobile which became affectionately known as the "Hupp".

Emile drove the Hupp to the restaurant where they relaxed over wine and ordered dinner. A small orchestra was playing a slow waltz, and several couples began to dance. Bonnie asked Emile for a dance. "Are you in the mood for a dance with your wife?"

"Honey, I'm going to sit quietly and enjoy the music. Why don't you ask our marine guest?"

Bonnie was disappointed and glanced at Carl. "What do you say, Carl?"

Carl placed his wine glass on the table and stood up, offering his hand to her. "It's been a long time since I danced. I'll try not to step on your toes."

Emile watched them on the floor, proud of his wife. She had tolerated the long hours that he had spent studying, yet she had been content living in Paris during his tour of duty at the war college. He watched Carl and Bonnie. Carl had whispered something in her ear as she turned to look at Emile sitting at the table, and then quickly broke eye contact. It was a simple thing, but it bothered Emile. He had a quiet jealous moment seeing how relaxed and comfortable they were in each other's arms.

He knew that Carl had a wife that had stayed at home while he attended the school. He rarely talked about her and Emile was careful not to ask him why she did not accompany him to Paris. Carl had been a frequent guest at Bonnie's and Emile's apartment. He was good company and fun to be with.

The waltz ended, and the couple made their way to the table with Emile. He was upset with himself for entertaining unpleasant thoughts about his wife and their new found friend. "Well," Emile exclaimed, standing as they sat down. "You two were a good-looking couple on the floor. I was never much of a dancer." He laughed at himself.

"Oh, Em, you do better than you let on," Bonnie smiled at him, grasping his hands in hers. "I see that our meals are being served."

"I'm hungry, too" Carl added. "The officer's mess at the college was not bad, but I'll be glad to be home with meals free of sauces."

"I'm sure your wife will be glad to see you again," Emile said. "Speaking of home, I propose a toast to the successful completion of a most difficult tour of duty."

"You and Bonnie have made this a much more pleasant tour than I imagined. Thanks to you both. My wife is anxious for my return to the states... We've had our differences and I'm hoping that we can resolve them. Our marriage is worth that effort, and I'm hoping that she wants that as much as I do."

It was the first time that Emile had heard him say anything about their marriage. They changed the subject and enthusiastically talked about their new assignments in Washington, D.C., promising to get together once they both settled into the Washington social scene. They relaxed over coffee and retired. Bonnie was anxious to settle Faye and Alpha in bed before it was too late. That was their last evening in France.

Emile had his Hupp stored on one of the large Army freighters that would take them home to the United States. They landed in Baltimore where they stayed in a hotel one evening while the Hupp and their luggage was off-loaded from the ship. Later, suitable quarters were located on the west side of the Potomac River in Arlington near Fort Meyers. This was the beginning of a tour of duty at the Capital that would last several years. Alpha and Faye would spend most of their childhood years in the city where they found it exciting.

Emile had a position on the Army general staff that was responsible for the development of plans to counteract any potential attacks against the nation or the territories it was responsible to defend. The experience he had received at Paris was put to good use. He liked his new position at the capital, but it demanded more spit and polish than most other posts. He handled that part with ease. It was the multitude of balls and parties on an almost nightly basis that he disliked. Almost every weekend was taken up by some event that required his presence. They ate out at some event more than they did at the apartment. He would have preferred to be at home with his family. Bonnie accompanied him to most events. She found them exciting and fun. He was promoted to the rank of major after serving a year in Washington.

Two years later, Emile and Bonnie met Carl and his wife at one of the impressive balls. Carl, too, had been promoted to the rank of Major and was looking forward to being sent to China. He and Carl talked a lot about the unsettled East and the rapid rise of militarism in Germany. These dark clouds foretold a future that worried every military officer who knew what was taking place. The United States had already demobilized the armed services so as to ease the financial burden on the country with a depression looming on the horizon.

The Army staff had to devise plans for any possible contingency, and do it with limited funds and resources. Their budgets had been dangerously cut. The country was woefully unprepared for war in any part of the world. Emile and the staff was worried that they could not defend the homeland against a determined attack. The military saw the danger and screamed for more resources, but none was forthcoming. The country was opposed to maintaining a large standing Army.

It was during this period that Emile and two other officers on the same staff were ordered to China to evaluate the situation. Japan was rattling its sabers again at China. They were given a twenty-four hour notice to get ready. Emile rushed to their apartment to tell Bonnie. He knew that it was not going to sit well with her. Their marriage was turning out to be a disappointment to both of them. They argued a lot about paying bills and the lack of funds to live a more carefree lifestyle. Bonnie was content going to parties and elaborate shows that were beyond their ability to afford. Some of the officers had family monies so that they could do those more expensive things. She occasionally berated Emile for not being in that more elite category.

Emile's prophecy that Bonnie was going to be outraged soon became reality. She was unhappy when he told her. Her first thought was that he should resign from the Army and get a job where they could be more in control of their lives. She was upset with the fact that she alone would have the burden of caring for the children while he was away.

"What you say is true, Bonnie. I can't change that. We both knew when we agreed to stay in the Army that these kinds of orders were routine. Many of our friends here in Washington are going through the same thing," he tried to explain and embraced her, understanding that it placed a burden on her as much as him.

She wrenched herself from his embrace and turned her back to him, trying to hide the rage that was consuming her. Then she turned to him with a determined tilt to her jaw and a frightening look in her eyes. "If you go to China, I won't be here when you get back."

"What do you mean you won't be here when I get back?" he snapped at her with a sick feeling in his stomach.

"Just what I said, Emile. We've come to a crossroads in our marriage. I'll take the children to my parents while you're gone and close down the apartment. We can settle things when you return. I want out, Emile."

He couldn't believe what she was saying. "You can't mean that, Bonnie!"

"Oh yes I do," she replied in a high-pitched voice. "It just isn't working for us or for the children. You have to admit that, Emile. We've just been going through the motions. I want to be in control of my life. The Army dictates our lives. Maybe that works for you, Emile, but it makes me feel like a puppet. This trip to China makes it easy."

"Easy for whom?" Emile screamed. "What about the kids? Don't they matter?"

"We can decide that on a more rational basis when you return," she replied. "Life just hasn't been fun anymore. Paris was fun and exciting. The Army expects too much from a family in Washington. I've been unhappy for a long time..."

Emile knew that was true. He had seen it slowly take place over the years. He was always apologizing for his choice of a career. She could never grasp what it meant to him to serve for a cause greater than the two of them. He gave up trying to explain what duty meant to him a long time ago.

"Well, if that's what you want, Bonnie," he answered. The conversation was making him weary and frightened. "Probably it's for the best that you visit your family for a while. I'll write to you and the kids at that address. I've got to pack my bag. The train to the coast leaves tonight in a couple of hours. Good-bye, Bonnie..."

She went to him and placed her arms around him. "Don't take it so hard, Em. We just never found that utopia we expected to find in our union. I'm as much to blame as you. You're a fine soldier, and I've always been proud of you, but, the discontent has reached a level where something must change. You have to admit that we never pulled the family wagon together very often. It was always a single effort, and that never satisfied either of us. Take care of yourself, Em. I'll keep you informed about events on the home front."

Emile said good-bye to Faye and little Alpha as he put them to bed. The last embrace with his Bonnie as he was going out the door left him angry and sad. It was a hell of a way to send a soldier off on a hazardous mission. He closed the door and climbed into a taxi overwhelmed with tears streaming down his face, relieved that it was dark enough to hide them from the driver.

He knew that his marriage had reached a level where both parties were discontented. Happiness and contentment were no longer shared by them. He reluctantly knew that when he returned from this mission, his life was going to change.

Chapter Eight

Eight Years Later

Emile sat in the family room of the rustic log cabin he had built the first year he had moved to Berlin, New Hampshire, in the majestic White Mountains, watching the flickering flames in the fireplace. He and Alpha had just finished cleaning up the kitchen from their traditional Sunday meal of ham and baked beans. Alpha had gone to his room upstairs to study. He was in his senior year at Berlin High School and was a good student. His sister Faye had stayed with her mother. It had been a mutually agreed arrangement that everyone was satisfied with. During the summer months, the two swapped places. Whenever it was possible the two shared the traditional holidays of Christmas, Thanksgiving, and birthdays together at whichever location it was agreed upon. They were very close and faithfully wrote to each other often, sharing events in their young lives.

Bonnie and Emile had separated in 1935 when he returned from his tour of duty in China. Their divorce was as amicable as possible for both parents wanted what was best for the two children. They had agreed to consult with each other about them and to make every effort to be mutually supportive of basic rules of behavior. Both parents agreed that the children should never be a part of their personal differences and both made efforts to apply the same rules of behavior. This latter agreement between Bonnie and Emile was rigidly adhered to without exception. Alpha and Faye accepted the guidelines and grew into courteous and respectful young adults. Bonnie was quick to remind them that the traditional virtues of Army life, duty, honor, self respect, and country, were worthy guides to a happy life, and that they should use their father as a good example. The arrangement avoided a lot of bitterness between the parents, and made it possible for them to put aside the differences that created the divorce. The two children found out early in the separation that they could not use one parent against the other to get what they wanted. Common sense, fair play, and compassion were the game rules that each parent used to raise the children.

Soon after the divorce, Emile resigned from the Army to take a job as a forester with the Brown Paper Company in Berlin, New Hampshire. At the same time he joined the New Hampshire National Guard and was pleased to learn that an opening was available for a major rate as an infantry battalion executive officer. He applied for it and was accepted. His experience in the last war had been an important factor in his selection. While he was away on summer training camp the two children stayed with Bonnie at her home in Burlington, Vermont. Their transition from one home to the other was seamless and was easy on everybody.

Emile's first duties as a forester for Brown Company allowed him to use his skills as a trained forestland manager to maintain a steady flow of pulpwood raw material without any depletion to the forest resource. In order to accomplish that important guideline, he established a large number of one-fifth acre sample plots within the vast acreage that reached into Maine, Vermont, and up to the Canadian boundary. Every tree within these growth plots was carefully tallied by specie, height, and diameter at breast height(dbh), four and a half feet. Increment borings were also taken to determine the rate of growth for the past ten years. With the above measurements at hand, it was possible for the forester to compute the amount of wood fiber within the sample plot. Those figures could be projected to give the forester a reasonably accurate average annual growth rate per acre per year.

This growth was treated by the forester much like interest in a bank account so that the average annual harvest of trees should always be less than the average annual growth. Good stewardship dictates that the plots be measured every five years so that an accurate annual harvest figure could be computed taking into consideration losses in the forest due to fire, disease, insect, and natural phenomenon. If the harvest is maintained at a rate less than the growth, then it will provide a constant supply of wood products forever. Foresters called it sustained yield.

Faye had shown great promise in high school. Both parents encouraged her to continue her education in a college of her choice. Emile had assured her that he could afford most any school except the expensive ivy league institutions. She chose Emile's alma mater, the University of New Hampshire. Faye entered college in 1939 and wanted to be a teacher, so she majored in education. Her brother and both parents were proud of the excellent grades she received in college. She was maturing into a serious young lady. She and her father had always been very close. That did not change after she entered college. She had a temperament more like her father than her mother. She was always proud of her dad's sense of fair play and decency. He had that soft, easy way about him that endeared him to those who knew him. His men in the National Guard held him in high regard for the same reasons. He was a natural leader who led by example instead of commands.

Emile and Alpha often visited with Faye on weekends. They went out to restaurants in the Dover and Portsmouth area and visited places along the Maine and New Hampshire coast. Their favorite location was the Nubble Lighthouse in York, Maine. They often sat on ledges and ate fried clams they had purchased at a small take-out on Route One known as El's Fried Clams.

Young Alpha and his sister, Faye, talked a lot on the phone after she started school in Durham. They shared their thoughts in letters to each other every week. Faye had been dating for a few years while Alpha was just thinking about it. They knew that their letters were private and would not be read by either parent unless they were requested to do so, therefore, they felt secure writing to each other how they felt about their dates and others they knew.

Alpha had written to Faye that he was going to join the Army as soon as he graduated from high school. The world was tearing itself apart, and the United States was scrambling to build up its armed forces which had been neglected for decades. The biggest horror for Emile and those who knew the truth was that the country would be drawn into a war with Japan and/or Germany before it was ready. It was already supplying arms and material to England. The U.S. Navy and Coast Guard were escorting convoys of ships to the British Isles, although the United States was a neutral nation on the explosive world scene.

Over the years Emile had avoided relationships with women. There had been numerous offers for him to date, but he had refused most of them. He did not want to be used the way Bonnie had taken advantage from the very beginning of their marriage. He was not lonely and had filled his life with the two children. In many ways he became closer to them after the divorce than he was prior to their breakup. The steady job at Brown Company helped in that respect.

Emile and Alpha often spent a weekend at their simple camp on Lake Hebron in Monson, Maine, where they had been fishing and swimming. It was a small cabin that his grandfather had built right after the war with Spain. It had been a happy meeting ground for family affairs while Emile was growing up. Aunts and uncles and cousins all had fond memories of the two room cabin with the upstairs like an Army barracks with privacy curtains around each bunk. Emile had spent a lot of time there after his divorce replacing the roof shingles and building a new one-hole outhouse. Every trip to the isolated cabin demanded that a certain amount of time had to be spent on maintenance and repairs. Everyone fondly remembers the mourning cry of the loons echoing across the lake. It was a primeval sound that touched the hearts of every person who experienced them. Their melancholic refrain helped Emile to get through a lot of ugly times in the war. The camp in the heart of Northern Maine was the one place where he could find peace and contentment. He was especially pleased to experience the tranquility and harmony with his son and daughter. They visited the enchanting cabin as often as they could, and they never failed to leave in a better frame of mind than when they arrived.

Emile thought often about a visit he and Alpha had made the summer of 1937 when Alpha was fourteen. They had closed up the camp and were driving on the gravel road between Abbot and Bingham, planning to eat a lunch of peanut butter and apple jelly sandwiches at a picturesque picnic spot on the Kennebec River at Bingham. They had been studying the heroic march in 1775 through the Maine wilderness by Benedict Arnold on his way to attack Quebec City. He was ordered by General Washington. Emile was an authority on the Revolutionary War and was always anxious to share his enthusiasm with Faye and Alpha.

They pulled into the small rest area beside the river with a canopy over a picnic table. It was the first trip to Maine they had made with his new 1936 Ford V/8 sedan. Emile was impressed with its performance. Alpha had just placed the large wicker picnic basket on the table when a 1932 Chevrolet coupe blew a tire on the road and pulled into the parking space beside their Ford. Emile had just removed a quart thermos bottle of coffee from the back seat when the tire burst. The noise startled him. The woman driving the coupe quickly pulled beside them under the trees and shut down the vehicle. She then placed her head in her arms on the steering wheel and seemed to be crying.

Emile rushed to the driver side of the coupe to see if the driver had been hurt. The window was down and she was shaking all over. "Are you hurt, Ma'am?" he asked, in a demanding voice.

She lifted her head to look at him through a veil of tears and shook her head negatively, reaching into her pocket to get a handkerchief.

"Do you have a spare?" he asked, checking the front left tire that had been shattered by some sharp object. The lady was driving a blue 1932 Chevrolet coupe with yellow wheels. It had two spare tire mounts on each front fender with a rear view mirror on top of them. Emile thought it looked brand new, it was so shiny and clean.

The lady took her time nervously blowing her nose and checking her purse that had fallen on the floor after her abrupt stop. She then turned to look at Emile and pointed to the tire on the right fender. "I know that one is new," she replied in a weak voice.

Emile checked the tire and asked Alpha to remove it from the mount. "My son and I will be pleased to change your tire for you, Ma'am. We had just stopped for lunch and have plenty of coffee and sandwiches," he said, pointing to the picnic table under the canopy. "You're welcome to share what we have."

The lady blew her nose again and wiped her eyes dry of tears with a clean handkerchief. "Thank you for being so helpful," she replied, getting out of the coupe to open the rumble seat cover. "The jack is in the rumble seat compartment."

Emile leaned over the side of the coupe to retrieve the jack and the handle. "Why don't you take a seat in the shade at the picnic table while my son and I change your tire. By the way, I'm Emile Ranta and this is my son, Alpha," he told her.

"I'm Cora Lambert," she replied, retrieving her purse on the seat of the coupe. I apologize for being such a bother. Thank you, Mr. Ranta, and you too, Alpha. That's a fitting name for a young man," she smiled.

"Thank you, Mrs. Lambert," he said, placing the jack beneath the front axle. "We'll have this fixed in no time."

Mrs. Lambert took a seat at the picnic table and watched the two methodically remove the old tire and insert the new one in its place. She was a middle-aged woman with streaks of gray hair pulled behind her ears with two barrettes. She was dressed in a light blue blazer and a plaid skirt. Her eyes reflected the anguish she could not hide, and they were glued on the rapid flow of the mighty Kennebec River beside her.

Emile and Alpha both saw the sad look in her eyes and thought it best to refrain from unnecessary conversation while they were changing the tires. When it was finished, Alpha carefully placed the jack in the rumble seat compartment and mounted the flat tire on the front fender while his father finished tightening the wheel lugs and replaced the hub cap.

Mrs. Lambert saw how well the two worked together and smiled as they approached the picnic table. "My, you two are efficient. Thank you so much for helping me. I must have hit a sharp edge of the curbing. I should have paid more attention to my driving."

"Every one makes mistakes, Mrs. Lambert," Emile told her taking a seat opposite her.

"That workout made me even more hungry," Alpha said, taking a seat next to Mrs. Lambert. "Would you like a cup of Dad's coffee and a peanut butter sandwich? Dad insists on making his own coffee." Alpha smiled at her. "He claims that mine is like troubled water."

She chuckled at his comments. She had a nice smile, but her eyes betrayed an inner turmoil she could not hide. "A cup of coffee will taste good. I haven't eaten for a while."

"We have something that is unique and tasty with coffee, Mrs. Lambert." Emile anxiously reached into the large picnic basket. He found what he was looking for and placed a small plate wrapped in wax paper in front of her. He unwrapped the paper and pointed to the rolls on the plate. "That is a treasured item made by the Swedes and Finns in Monson, Maine, where I was born and raised. We call it a bulla roll, and I get a supply whenever I return to the town. I hope you like it, Ma'am."

"I can smell the cardamom seeds in it already," she replied, taking a small bite of the pastry. "It has a subtle sweet taste, Mr. Ranta, I understand your addiction to them. Thank you for sharing it with me."

"You're welcome," he answered, pleased that she also found the secret to their favorite food when he was growing up in the small town. He looked at her coupe and turned to her. "You have one of the most attractive coupes on the road, Mrs. Lambert. The color scheme is really nice."

"I needed a vehicle and selected it on a spur of the moment. It turned out to be a wise one. It's fun to drive. I needed a reliable automobile to do my work," she explained, taking another bite from her bulla. "These are delicious. Thank you for being so kind and thoughtful."

"My son and I are on our way back to Berlin, New Hampshire."

Mrs. Lambert noticed that Emile was wearing some of his Army dungarees and asked, "Are you in the Army?"

"I was considering a career in the Army until a good job was offered to me as a forester for the Brown Company in Berlin. I still attend National Guard training sessions to maintain military skills," he replied, surprised that he was relating that much information to a stranger.

She smiled again. "You have that presence of an Army man," she told him. "I'm a nurse and work for the State of Maine assisting rural families. That's why I needed a reliable vehicle. I was an Army nurse in the last war."

"I can honestly tell you, Mrs. Lambert, that the Army nurses are the most respected personnel in the service. I speak as a person who has been wounded twice in combat and been nursed back to health by nurses like you. You've earned my respect and admiration, Ma'am."

She shyly answered him in a soft voice. "Thank you for such a compliment. It's nice to know that our work is appreciated. Well, I've finished my coffee and that delicious bulla roll, and I should be on my way. I'm anxious get to an elderly Indian lady in Harmony who broke her leg in a bad fall a few days ago. She's not doing very well. The local doctor is out of town on a vacation, so she depends on me to care for her."

Emile had been studying the lady. She was about his age with a slender build. She was hiding a lot of pain. It shown in her deep set eyes with dark lines. She smiled some, but it was not easy for her to do so. She seemed alone and had a forlorn air about her that touched him. Even Alpha noticed that.

"I understand," Emile replied, finishing a cup of coffee.

She excused herself and stood up to walk to her coupe. Emile and Alpha walked with her. Emile opened the door of the coupe for her to enter. "It's been a privilege, Mrs. Lambert. You're an angel of mercy, and I wish you well."

"That goes for me, too," added Alpha.

"Thank you for being so helpful," she said, embracing Emile, and then quickly got into the coupe. She started the Chevrolet and waved as she left the parking area.

Chapter Nine

Faye and Alpha had talked a lot about their parent's divorce and how each reacted to it. Both had agreed that their mother felt no remorse about the breakup of a family. As a matter of fact, her marriage to a handsome marine officer shortly after the divorce was finalized, had seemed too quick. The contrast between their father and mother was extreme. Bonnie had seemed happy after her recent marriage, and she went out of her way to make the transition easy for all concerned.

Emile accepted the divorce with silence, wishing Bonnie happiness that he was not able to provide and was unable to find himself. Bitterness had become a frequent part of his outlook on life. They both worried about him. Emile became more of a loner than ever. He frequently had that forlorn stare into space that frightened them. Alpha told his sister that he had seen a distinct change in their father's attitude and demeanor after they had changed a tire for a lady.

When Alpha and his father reached Berlin after the trip to Monson, Alpha got his things together so that he could trade places with Faye for a portion of the summer. Two weeks later in August, Emile had to leave with his National Guard battalion for training exercises. Most of the time they went to Canada to train with the Canadian Army in New Brunswick. This year they were going to Fort Devens in Massachusetts. While he was away the two stayed together with Bonnie.

That summer of 1937, Faye was able to get her driving license in Maine when she was with her father. Shortly after that, her father brought her to Vermont to her mother's house and let her drive his Ford most of the distance. He complimented her on doing a good job of driving. "Maybe your mother will let you drive their Buick. You'll see a big difference from this Ford."

"Lewis let me drive it some this spring. He wasn't very patient with me when I made a mistake," she shared with him.

"Give him a chance, Honey," her father suggested. "All of us have to adapt to the changes in our lives. It'll work out in time."

She turned to look into her father's face and asked directly:

"What about you, Father? How have you adapted? I haven't seen you smile much since the divorce. Mother seems happy, but you still seem angry."

"How can one react differently? The divorce was your mother's choice, not mine. I agreed because I knew for a long time that she was discontented and wanted out. I gave it to her because I loved her, and it was something she wanted. I knew there was someone else, and that really hurt. I don't want to sound like a cry-baby, but I just haven't been able to adapt to being so harshly discarded like an old shoe. Sorry, Honey. I didn't mean to lay all the blame on your mother. I, too, was just as responsible by staying in the Army. She hated it for a long, long time."

Faye hoped that she was not out of line by telling him what Alpha had told her about the lady with the flat tire. "Alpha said that you seemed a little less distant than you have been, and that you were more relaxed while talking with her."

"What are you trying to say, Honey? I saw in the lady with the flat tire the same torment that I've been harboring, and it made me feel that I'm not the only one to be dominated by sorrow. She was carrying a horrible burden with courage, determination, and compassion. I admire those virtues in people. If you were looking for a response from me, now you have it, Honey. I'm not a fickle teenager when it comes to women."

"We both know that, Dad. You never talk about your feelings or things that make you happy. It's just that we love you and want you to enjoy life. You deserve better than what you have now," Faye kissed her father on the cheek.

That first night in Berlin, Faye had told her father that several boys in school had asked her for a date. He smiled at her and said, "Well, Honey, you're a very attractive young lady, and young men like attractive girls. Your mother was the prettiest girl in school when I first dated her. My only advice to you is to choose your companions with care. Let that little voice that's inside of you be your best guide."

"Dad," Faye was quick to ask, "Do you still love Mom?"

"You're full of questions tonight, aren't you? You've touched on something I'm not prepared to answer right now. I'm still angry that your mother was so anxious to get the divorce. We differed a lot about the way the Army does things. As I told you earlier, her rejection is the hardest to bear. I never cheated on your mother and never was unfaithful to our vows."

"I don't want to upset you, Dad, but I have a question that's been on my mind for a long time." She swallowed and avoided his penetrating eyes. "Do you ever think of me as being the daughter of another man?" She knew that she was going to hurt him, but she had to have an answer. That fact had haunted her, even when she was very young.

As she had predicted, he was stung by the question. He answered it with one of his own, "Have I ever given you cause to doubt my love for you, Faye?"

She rushed to kneel before his chair and embraced him. "Oh, Father, forget that I asked such a cruel question. Forgive me... Lately, I've been thinking a lot about him..."

"This conversation is getting heavy, dear daughter," he explained, worried that she would be concerned about her self-worth. The two hurtful questions: Who was her real father, and what kind of a man was he? They were important because she contained his genes within her body, and she was troubled by that fact. Emile understood her desire to know. He would have the same impulse if he was her.

"Listen, dear daughter," he calmly embraced her, "Yes, I know how who your paternal father is. I can honestly tell you that he was a friend of mine that I trusted and respected. He was killed in the war. Sure, you have inherited some of his genetic makeup, but you know that environment has a greater influence on who we are than the genes do. If you can, dear girl, put those dark thoughts out of your mind. I swear that I've never thought of you as anything except my dearest daughter whom I'm so proud of."

Faye stored every word in her memory bank. This was unchartered territory for both of them. She sat back in her chair as he continued.

"No young lady is loved more than I love you, just as I do Alpha. When your mother first told me about her condition, I was outraged at her unfaithfulness. That had nothing to do with you, Faye. The consequences of that act was uniquely on your mother's shoulders. At first I wanted to end the marriage, but when your mother told me that she was entertaining an abortion, I was against it. I was able to accept her condition, and I have never regretted it. You must believe that, Faye. It's the truth. My first visit into the hospital the day you were born, you reached out and grasped my thumb with your little dimpled fingers. A thrill went through my body, and at that moment, I made a vow to love you and to keep you from harm in every way possible, dear child. Don't ever forget that. The fact that you wonder about your paternal father is only natural. Watching you grow into the lovely young lady you've become has given me a wonderful sense of joy and pride. I'm a lucky Dad. Now, Honey, end of conversation, ok?"

"End of conversation," she replied with tears forming in her eyes. "I'm the lucky one. Thanks for being such a wonderful Dad."

The summer of 1941 Emile saw an increased awareness on the part of the military leaders of the country. Unrest in Asia and Europe made them realize that the nation was not strong enough to oppose a determined attack against the United States. Therefore, congress was allotting more and more funds for weaponry and a desperately needed increase in soldiers and sailors. The Army and Navy still went into training sessions with the same weaponry they used in 1918, eighteen years ago. There was much work to be done. Emile welcomed the increased tempo of training for the National Guard and the Reserves. For annual summer maneuvers his infantry battalion was ordered to Fort Devens in Massachusetts where they joined other New England units to form a full division.

Efforts were made to increase manpower. The existing Guard and Reserve units were valuable resources. They could release platoons and companies of trained units that would act as a nucleus to which untrained men were added to form battalions and regiments. The trained existing formations were the most valuable resource of the country. All existing formations were ordered to provide those well-trained units for the express purpose of developing larger units. Fresh new divisions were being formed all across the country. This massive increasing of formations meant an increase in officers to command them, and promotions were increasing to keep up with the demand. Emile was given command of a full battalion with a rank of Lieutenant Colonel. His battalion was given a fleet of new Ford one-and-a-half-ton trucks prior to their order to travel to Fort Devens for summer training.

Once they arrived in Fort Devens they were assigned to an ad hoc division and participated in large-scale maneuvers. They were ordered to reinforce a portion of the Massachusetts Atlantic shore. They were to move all of their men and equipment in whatever means of transportation was available to them. Trains, trucks, and buses were used to deploy the division with the coastal artillery units to repel an attack against the Massachusetts coast.

One platoon of military police had not received adequate information about the route in which Emile's battalion was to take; therefore, they were ordered through a cranberry bog that still had standing water in it. Several of the Ford trucks got stuck in the mud. Those vehicles that had winches on them had to be used to retrieve the trucks. Suddenly one of the winch lines snapped under excessive pressure and severely cut three soldiers in the legs.

The full division had an Army mobile field hospital attached that had already been set up close to the shoreline in an open field. Emile called his regimental command post for directions to the field hospital and was told that it was already set up to receive patients. He ordered the three injured men to be taken there in a Dodge vehicle that he was using for a command post. He had to finish inserting his battalion in the line of defense assigned to him, and planned to visit the men in the hospital later.

He saw to it that the men were prepared to respond to any threat. Emile was satisfied with their deployment. He had also formed a fire brigade out of twenty infantrymen on a Ford truck so that they could respond to any front that was threatened. His division general was pleased with the way he inserted his battalion. Experienced leadership was helping to show those with little or no experience how things are done. Emile's battalion was on display for the entire division, and he was in his element!

That evening he attended an officer's conference at a large tent where the performance of every unit within the division was discussed and evaluated. The essence of the large formation was to maintain a strong presence on the coast for forty-eight hours. Emile's men had drawn ammunition and food for two days in the field. They were to return to Fort Devens in force and full division formation.

After the conference, Emile located the position of the mobile field hospital so that he could visit the men that were injured. He was given a staff sedan to make the trip inland a few miles to the hospital. The three men had been treated soon after their arrival at the tent and were glad to see their commander. Their wounds were mostly superficial, and they would be able to join their units for the return trip to Devens. He chatted with them as was his way and explained how the battalion was spread across several miles of coast. They appreciated his concern for their welfare, and he left to check with the nurse on duty that evening.

He located the nurse station and announced himself to a nurse at a desk. "Hello, I'm Colonel Ranta. I just wanted to make sure that my men have been good patients."

Another nurse who had been unpacking a shipping box heard what he had said and turned to him. "Colonel Ranta, haven't we met before, Sir?"

Emile instantly recognized her even in the poor light of the tent. "Yes, I remember, Captain. What a coincidence. So you're also one of our Army nurses."

"Yes, I've been in the Reserves for two years. My husband was a career officer. After he passed away, it was an honor for me to make some contribution, Colonel," she replied.

"The Army Nurse Corps is the most respected unit in the service for good reason. I personally can vouch for that."

A third nurse interrupted them. "We have orders to remain in place until we discharge our patients. Captain Lambert, why don't you take the evening off? You've been on duty for twenty-four hours. We've got things under control. Lieutenant Walsh can take over for the evening."

Emile listened carefully to what was said and turned to Captain Lambert. She still had that sad, forlorn look on her face that he recalled from their first meeting beside the Kennebec River. "Captain Lambert, I'm leaving the hospital now. I have an Army sedan available outside. May I give you a lift to your quarters?"

She made some notations on a pad of paper and dropped the pen. "I am tired, Colonel. I don't want to be a bother."

"Lady, I'm not in the habit of making offers I don't mean. It'll be my pleasure to escort you to any place you want to go. I also have the evening free. My three soldiers are in good hands, so I don't have to worry about them."

Captain Lambert was dressed in dungaree fatigues and asked him, "I want to get out of these coveralls. Give me a few minutes to change, and I'll join you."

"Take your time, Ma'am. I'll be waiting at the tent entrance."

"I won't be long."

Ten minutes later she appeared dressed in her tan summer uniform. Emile saw her and got out of the sedan to open the door for her. "Thank you for offering to see me to our quarters. They're down the road a few miles." She pointed to the south.

"This training session has been great experience for everybody involved. We've still got a lot to learn, but exercises like this will help if for no other reason than to point out our errors. I think our local National Guard units deployed well," Emile explained.

She listened to his evaluation of the situation and anxiously asked, "Do you think we'll be pulled into a war?"

"To be real honest, yes. After what I saw in my tour of duty in China, I personally view Japan as the greatest threat. Their army is well trained, well disciplined, and is led by fanatical zealots who are as vicious as I've ever seen," he paused as she pointed to a tent off the side of the road in a large field.

He pulled into the field beside the tent. "I hope that I didn't alarm you with my strong opinions, Captain. It's nice to see a familiar face. Thanks for taking such good care of my men."

"Your soldiers were model patients, Colonel. Thanks for the ride. I still remember that time you helped me with a flat tire. That was a particularly difficult time for me. My husband died after a heroic battle with lung cancer. He was a doctor and there was nothing to do but wait for the end. I was by his side to that cruel end. All I could do was make him as comfortable as possible. I think that those last few months together were the best moments in our marriage. Now he's with the angels free of pain..."

The description of her husband's death explained the pain she carried in her eyes. "Your husband was a lucky man to have you for a wife. I didn't mean to dredge up painful memories, Captain. There has to be some comfort in the fact that he's in a much better place and is free of pain. I'm sure that he looks upon your work as a nurse with pride and affection. Love does not die with the physical body. You're fortunate to have the gift of such warm memories."

He opened the door and came around to her side of the sedan. "May I escort you to the entrance of the tent?"

"Yes," she replied in a low voice. "It has been nice seeing you again, Colonel. Thanks for the lift."

"It's been my pleasure, Ma'am. May I take the liberty of asking to see you again when maneuvers are over? I'll be going up to Monson again for a few days with my daughter and son. You've already met my son, Alpha."

"What about your wife, Colonel?" she asked directly.

"Our marriage was not a happy one, and I take the blame for that by staying in the Army after the war in France. We divorced a few years ago," he was glad to explain.

"I understand," she replied. "We can exchange addresses and phone numbers when you come tomorrow to check on your men, ok?"

"That sounds great to me. May I call you Cora instead of Captain Lambert?"

"I was going to ask you the same thing," she smiled. "Otherwise I'd feel that I had to salute a superior officer all the time. This has been a nice encounter, Emile. Thank you." With that she gently kissed him on the cheek and disappeared into the tent.

Chapter Ten

Emile was sitting on a ledge formation beside the beach on the Massachusetts coast drinking a cup of coffee from a regimental field kitchen set up a few yards inland. He loved the sea as much as he did the forest. Both gave him a quiet sense of solitude and peace. He had been watching two small Coast Guard patrol boats close to shore. They were a part of the military training exercise, too.

A female voice called him. "Colonel Ranta."

He turned to see Cora Lambert walking towards him. "Hello."

"I wasn't sure it was you. The men at the field kitchen told me you were on the beach."

"I'm surprised," he greeted her with a smile. "I see that you got a cup of coffee. The Army still runs on coffee."

"It tastes good. I was called back to duty shortly after you dropped me off. Two artillery men were injured and needed care. I stayed on for the night and just got off. I don't often have a chance to enjoy the seashore, so I thought I'd stroll down to the beach with a hot coffee."

"Come, have a seat," he pointed to the ledge. "There's room for both of us."

She sat with her feet dangling over the edge staring at the water. "If war does come, it will take a brutal toll of young men's lives," she declared in a whisper and shuddered. "I don't like to think how bad it will be."

"Every soldier thinks the same thing, Cora. Have you had any breakfast?" he asked.

"I've finished my coffee. A refill will be appreciated," she answered.

Emile stood up on the ledge and hollered to the men on the nearby field kitchen to bring over more coffee and whatever they have that's sweet and hot. A young sergeant responded instantly with a thermos of coffee, sugar, cream, and a plate of warm apple turnovers.

Emile thanked the sergeant and placed the tray between him and Cora on the ledge. He grinned, "Rank does have its advantages." He noted that Cora did not show as much sadness in her eyes as she did last evening. "What are your plans after this exercise is over?"

She took a big bite out of a warm apple turnover and swallowed. "I'll go back to Skowhegan where my rural nurse office is located. My friends have taken over for me while I attend annual training exercises like this with the Maine National Guard. What about you, Emile?"

"As soon as we get our gear stored away in Berlin I'll be going back to Monson at an old family camp on Lake Hebron for a few days of fishing. These are unsettled times, and tomorrow is never a sure thing, Cora. Therefore, I'm going to be bold and tell you that I'd like to see more of you if possible. If I've offended you, I'm sorry, but I voiced what I honestly feel."

She listened to his words. The short interludes she had shared with him had been pleasant, and she felt that he was a sincere person. "It has been almost two years since my husband died. I can honestly tell you that there are times when his memory is overwhelming, and tears flow easily. I cannot deny that..."

"And I'm not asking you to, Cora. It's a tribute to the union you two shared. Your husband very likely is your guardian angel. I'm sure that he would like to see you happier than you have been. I have no intention of forcing myself upon you if you're not ready to meet new friends. If what I ask is too soon, then I withdraw it and wish you all the best, Cora."

He placed his coffee cup on the tray and poured coffee from the thermos. "Would you like more coffee?"

"Yes, please, Emile. I'm flattered by your request to see me again. I'm almost fifty years old."

"Since when has youth had a monopoly on feelings from the heart?" he snapped back at her. "I'm forty-nine and that has nothing to do with what I asked of you. I did not mean to hurt you, Cora, or to dredge up old hurtful feelings." He was prepared to leave the beach and turned towards the open sea with the coffee cup in his hand. "I'm afraid I asked for too much too soon, and I apologize. Now I've got to get back to my battalion."

She saw the dejection on his face and reached out to him with beseeching hands. "Emile, do not be angry with me. I merely wanted you to know more about me..."

"Lady, don't you get weary fighting the world alone?"

"Oh yes, yes, I do, Emile. Searching for something worthwhile to fill up the long, lonely hours of each day has consumed me. It has been comforting to be able to call you a friend. It's all so sudden. I don't know how to handle it... help me, oh God, there has to be more to life than what I've experienced these past two years..."

Emile placed his coffee cup on the ledge and turned to her. Emotionally she was a lady on the edge of a cliff and was about to jump off. He reached out for her. She quickly entered his arms. He prayed that their embrace on the shore marked the end of sleepless nights and long days filled with emptiness for her. They were two lonely people searching for something meaningful to fill the hours with something better than they had been experiencing.

"Hold me, Emile, help me... help me..." He heard her plea and wrapped his arms tightly around her. It was a moment in his life that he would never forget. Two lonely hearts searching for meaning in their lives had come together at a time and place neither had anticipated.

Cora wept in his embrace and in a weary voice beseeched her God to hear her plea for release from the pain. Time stood still for them. Emile was frightened that the lady in his arms was having an emotional breakdown. Spasmodic ripples ran through her body. He felt her knees shaking and was about to lay her down on the sand when, suddenly, her deep erratic breathing stopped, and her body relaxed against him.

"Cora... Cora," he called in her ear. "You're frightening me, and I don't know how to help you. Please answer me!"

She laid her head against his chest. He could smell the soft scent of heliotrope in her hair, and she was slowly bracing her feet to stand on her own. She then lifted her head and looked into his eyes. They relaxed and withdrew from the embrace.

"Lady, you gave me a scare, and I feel responsible for your reaction to my request. I apologize for assuming too much too soon. Here, sit on the ledge for a moment, please."

He helped to lift her onto the ledge. She reached into her pocket for a handkerchief and blew her nose and dried her eyes. He checked the thermos bottle and gave her a full cup of fresh coffee, putting in cream and sugar for her.

"Here, maybe a warm cup will make you feel better." He carefully placed the cup in her hands.

She took two sips from the steaming cup and placed it on the ledge. "Thank you," she said, avoiding his intense stare. "I'm sorry that you had to witness my emotional outburst. Do not worry, I'm okay. I don't want to keep you from your battalion. This is a poor place for personal problems to be aired. You may not believe, it but I feel better. Sharing an early morning coffee with you has triggered emotions and feelings that have held me in bondage for the past two years."

He listened carefully to her words and thought that, perhaps, he had witnessed a catharsis. She seemed much more in control of herself.

She continued, placing her hand on his arm. There was a soft gentle air about her that he had not seen before. "Earlier this summer when you and your son changed my flat tire, I left the scene with a warm appreciation for your unselfish offer of help. I had seen in your eyes the same pain that I was experiencing and I really thought that it would be nice to have a friend like you. As time passed, those thoughts gave me bad feelings, and I punished myself for letting them interfere with my mourning for my dead husband. It was as if thoughts of you were replacing memories and feelings for him. I blamed myself for being unfaithful to his memory. Am I making any sense, Emile?"

"More than you know, Cora. Thanks for sharing those thoughts with me. I can honestly tell you that I also had been thinking about our chance meeting on the road. A lovely lady with a cute blue Chevrolet coupe had made my day complete." He smiled, relieved to tell her.

She heard him and returned his smile, jumping off the ledge.

"Now, Colonel, you've got to get back to your battalion. Your men need you. Thanks for being so kind and patient with me. Will I see you again before the end of the exercise?"

Amazed at the difference in the lady's demeanor, he replied, "Yes, I'll look you up before we leave the coast. Is your medical unit going back to Fort Devens?"

"No, we're being released when orders from Division arrive so that we can return directly to Maine. I'll have a few days before I have to report to the Rural Nurse Association in Skowhegan."

"I'll look you up before we leave, Lady," he grabbed her by the arm and escorted her to the medical tent.

"Thanks for being such a good listener, Emile," she told him, kissing him on the cheek. "And thanks for being a friend when I really needed one."

He turned to leave and waved at her. He had a feeling that something special had happened to him that morning. The little voice inside of him also cautioned him to not ask for too much too soon.

They did meet again. Emile's battalion was the last unit to leave the coast. He caught Cora just as they were finished packing supplies and equipment into new Army GMC ten-wheeler trucks. She was getting ready to climb aboard the last truck in the convoy. They exchanged addresses and telephone numbers with the promise of getting together shortly after Labor Day. It was a brief encounter, and Emile whispered in her ear, "I look forward to next time. You take care of yourself. Give yourself the same kind of attention you give to your patients, promise?"

"I promise, Colonel Ranta. Until we meet again," she replied, gently kissing him.

He had helped her climb into the rear of the last truck and stood beside the road waving until it turned a corner out of sight. A lonely feeling crept over him. Tomorrow was filled with happy potential, yet dark shadows were descending upon the country. They made him feel selfish that he was only thinking of himself. The country was about to be tempered by fire so powerful and destructive that it frightened him. He thought of his son, Alpha, who was about to join the Army. Dark clouds wiped away any joy that he may have had about Cora. The Army that he loved was the only institution that stood in the way of the powerful and brutal Axis blitzkrieg that was eating up smaller nations in both Europe and Asia. He knew better than most how terribly unprepared they were to confront the powerful enemies. That thought left no room for personal joy or happiness.

Chapter Eleven

Emile thanked the men in the battalion for their excellent performance during the summer training period. He was proud of them and they knew that it was genuine. There was an air of apprehension for the future that transcended most people's thoughts. The men knew as well as Emile that war clouds were gathering in Asia and in Europe. The United States could not stand alone against two countries with the most powerful armies and navies in the world. Therefore, they took their training exercises seriously and were glad to have such an experienced Army officer as their commander.

The day that Emile arrived back in Berlin with his battalion, Alpha met him at the armory with the Ford. He had some news he was anxious to share with his dad. He had already called his mother to inform her. He threw his father's duffel bag in the back seat of the Ford and took his place behind the wheel to drive him home.

"I have some news, Dad. I joined the Army while you were on maneuvers."

The news was not unexpected, but it hit Emile hard. His first thoughts fixed on the fact that his son was no longer a child, but a young man capable of making his own decisions. Emile knew what combat was like and was frightened for his son. There was no way he could protect him from that trauma, and it gave him a sick, churning feeling in his gut that he could not control.

"Well, son," Emile studied him at the wheel of the car. "I knew it was coming. Have you told your mother?"

"Yes, I called her two nights ago."

"When do you have to report to the recruiting center?" Emile asked with a tightness in his throat.

"They told me it would be within a couple of days. I'll be going to Fort Dix in New Jersey."

"Are you sure this is what you want, son?"

"I know that you have reservations about my joining. We've talked a lot about it this past summer. I didn't want to wait for the draft. Even if I had signed up for college, I would have been called by the draft. I want to do my part, Dad, just the way you've been doing all of your life."

"I understand, son," Emile told him. "I had thought we could get in another fishing trip up to the camp, but these uncertain times are setting different priorities for the whole country."

"I've been thinking about that, and I wanted you to be proud of me. A lot of my friends in school have family members in your battalion and they all have nice things to say about you as their commanding officer. I hope to emulate that legacy of leadership you've given to me and Faye."

Alpha pulled the Ford into the driveway. Emile walked around the car to embrace his son. "No man was ever more proud of his son than I am of you right now. Be yourself and you'll do just fine, Alpha. My, you'll look good in the uniform. The Ranta family has a long tradition of being soldiers."

Two days later, Emile drove Alpha to the recruiting office and watched him climb aboard an Army bus. It was one of the most emotional days in his life. His little boy had grown into manhood almost overnight!

The house he returned to was empty, and a melancholic feeling overwhelmed him. Tears slowly formed in his eyes as he dialed the phone. He had promised Alpha that he would call Faye to tell her the news. He had taken her to Burlington to be with her mother while she was on summer vacation and he was on maneuvers. She had only one more semester to go before she received her degree and certificate in education.

The phone rang three times before Faye answered the phone. "Hello?"

"Hi, Faye, this is Dad. I wanted to let you know that your brother is now on his way to an Army training center in New Jersey. He sends his love. You and your brother have been the joys of my life. How are things with you, Honey? When do you want me to come and get you?"

"You can come anytime, Dad. The sooner the better. I have a job in the library and they want me to come a few days early for indoctrination and to see how the system works."

"That should be good experience for you, Honey. Would you mind if I come to Vermont to get you now? I just dropped off Alpha, and it'll give me something to do. We could stop at a nice restaurant to have supper on our return trip."

"Today will be great for me. You sound a little down, Father. Now you know how we worry about you when you are on duty. I love you. Mother wants to talk to you."

"Hello, Emile," Bonnie soberly announced. "I just wanted to tell you that I'm so worried about Alpha. He's just a kid, and the way things in the world look he might even be in combat soon."

"That's true, Bonnie, but you're wrong about his being a kid. He's a man, and he'll make us proud, you wait and see. It's normal for us to hate to see him go off on his own. Don't forget that we were that same age a few years ago and experienced a war. Try not to worry, Bonnie, he's in more competent hands than you imagine. I'm coming directly for Faye and will see you in a couple of hours."

"Thanks for calling, Emile."

When he arrived at Burlington, he was greeted by a daughter who was anxious to leave the household. Later, on the road back home, they stopped at a restaurant in Montpelier. Faye had been unusually quiet.

"Is something wrong, Faye?"

They ordered their meals, and Faye looked into her father's penetrating eyes. "Dad, you might as well know that Mom's marriage is not going well."

"I thought your mother was a little quieter than usual," he replied.

"The problem is Lewis. He drinks a lot and often stays out at night with the guys. On those times that I was alone with him, like when Mom went shopping for groceries, he made me feel uncomfortable with his looks. He seemed to undress me with his eyes. He often remarks that I'm growing up quick, and he touches me with a familiarity that frightens me, Dad. I was glad to get your call," she confessed.

Her description of Bonnie's husband did not surprise him. "The next time I see him, I'll teach him some manners. Does your mother know about this, Faye?"

"I haven't said anything to her. Maybe she sees it and is unable to do anything, but she has not talked to me about it. She's not happy, Dad."

"Maybe you better stay in New Hampshire more, Faye," suggested her father. "I'm not sure when I'll be called to active duty. These are unsettled times, and I expect it very soon. Maybe I'll be called before the battalion is activated. I'm sure they can use my experience in helping to get this country prepared for the onslaught that's aimed straight at us."

Faye sighed and looked into his deep-set eyes. "Are things really that bad, Father? It blows my mind to think that both you and Alpha will be in the Army at the same time. I know that mother is worried about that too."

"You must know, Honey, that I've spent most of my adult life in the service of our country, and I consider it a privilege, not a burden. I think your brother feels the same way. What do you say if we have a piece of homemade custard pie after our meal? I'm going to have another cup of coffee."

She smiled at him. "You haven't changed, Dad. A cup of coffee and a piece of custard pie have always been a favorite with you. I'll join you."

As they were walking out to the Ford, he handed the keys to Faye. "How about chauffeuring your old dad the rest of the way home? When I'm called, you should use the Ford, Faye. I just put new tires on it and changed the muffler. The engine runs great. It's got about forty thousand miles on it, so it should give you reliable transportation for a while."

"What do you want me to do about the house in Berlin, Dad?" She was beginning to feel responsible for keeping their home the way they all remembered it. She knew it was important for anyone in the armed services.

"For now, until you complete this coming semester, you should plan on keeping the house open. After that, it all depends on where you'll be getting a place to teach school,

Faye. Don't worry about it now. Things have a way of working themselves out. The best situation would be for you to get a job in or near Berlin and you could live at the house.

"I've already paid for your tuition, room, and board at the dormitory for this semester," Emile informed his daughter. "Do you want to come to the house or go directly to the college?"

"I left some things I'll need at home, Dad. Would it be too much for you to bring me back to the university tomorrow? That way I'll have all of my clothes and other paraphernalia for the semester."

"Sure, we can do that. How are you fixed for pocket money, Honey?

"Mom has been saving some money that Lewis didn't know about, and she gave me fifty dollars," she said.

"Don't let me forget to give you the household checkbook when we get home. I really expect to get a phone call any day for recall to active duty, so you may as well be prepared to take care of the bills that come in and use what you need from the checking account. My salary with Brown Company comes directly to the checking account. I will mail my paychecks to you so that you can deposit them in the bank. When I'm called, I'll have my Army salary processed the same way. So, you'll have plenty of money. Maybe I'll have to give it an audit on occasion," he laughed.

She laughed with him. "What if I go on a spending spree and use it all up?"

"Then, young lady, you'll experience my wrath which some soldiers have told me can be frightening." They both laughed at each other. Faye was proud of him. His modest, caring ways made him a wonderful role model. They were lucky to have him.

The next day Faye and her father loaded all of her things into the Ford and they drove back to the university. He helped her carry her things into her room at Fairchild Hall. It took several trips. One of her favorite pieces of furniture was an orange crate she had painted blue and used as a bed stand where she kept her Baby Ben alarm clock.

"The next time we do this, maybe I should bring the company truck," he joked with her.

She warmly embraced him. "Thanks for everything, Dad, but most of all for being your kind and caring self. My dorm number is the same as I've had for the past years."

"Good luck, Honey," he said, holding her close to his heart. "I'll see you next weekend, but don't be surprised if you see me sooner. I have a feeling it's going to be days instead of weeks."

"I'll pray for you and Alpha, Dad," she told him as he got behind the wheel of the Ford. "Thanks for giving me the responsibility for the house. I won't let you down. I'm proud of you, Dad," she waved as he pulled onto the street. Tears ran down her cheeks. She could not imagine a life without him.

Emile picked up Route 16 and headed north from Durham. He had seen the moisture in Faye's eyes as he left. It was a sad time for him also. His baby girl and baby boy were grown and were taking on the responsibilities of adults. That pleased him and frightened him at the same time. He thought about Bonnie's husband, Lewis, and was relieved that Faye would not have to face his boorish habits once he was called to duty. The closer he drove towards North Conway, the more he thought about Cora Lambert. He reviewed all that had taken place those two days at the coast, and he admitted to himself that he was attracted to the lady. Knowing that he may not have a lot of time, he decided to give her a call at Skowhegan soon after he arrived home.

He took Route 16 north through the White Mountains, arriving home two hours after he had dropped Faye off at Durham. His first impulse was to call Cora at the number she had given him.

She answered the phone, "Hello."

"Hello, Cora, this is Emile Ranta calling. I just placed my daughter, Faye, in school. She has one more semester before she gets her certificate in education. The house seems empty. My son has left for basic training at Fort Dix, New Jersey. I enjoyed our time together at the coast on maneuvers. How are things for you?"

"It's good that you called, Emile. I still have some time off from my civilian job. The commander of our Army mobile hospital unit warned us to put our personal affairs in order because he expects the unit will be called to full active duty soon."

"I'm waiting for the same kind of orders, Cora," Emile added. "It doesn't look good for the country. I pray that we can increase our preparedness and industrial capacity in time to meet the roller coaster that's aimed at us. I'm calling to see if I could come down to see you again. We could go out to eat at your favorite restaurant. What do you say?"

"When we said good-bye at the coast I wondered if we would ever meet again, Emile. The answer to your question is yes, I'm free and will enjoy your company. I know a really good Italian restaurant here in Skowhegan. What time do you suggest? It's about sixty miles from Berlin to Skowhegan on Route 2."

"I can be there by noon tomorrow. I have your address. Thanks for accepting the invitation. I'll see you tomorrow."

"Thanks for calling, Emile."

When he arrived at her house the next morning, she was beside the garage washing her Chevy coupe. She saw him turn into the driveway and turned off the water.

"You made good time." She greeted him with a smile. "My coupe was dirty, so I washed it."

"Hi, Cora," he replied. "That's a cute vehicle."

She had her hair covered with a kerchief tied under her chin and had a pair of Army coveralls on. "Come in the house for a moment while I get out of these dungarees."

It was a small Cape Cod house with one dormer over the driveway. "You have a nice home," he exclaimed, entering the small living room with a large fireplace on the north wall.

"Make yourself comfortable, Emile," she said, motioning to the couch in front of the fireplace.

"You take your time, Lady."

He checked a portrait of Cora with a man he assumed to be her husband. He stood up to look closer. He was three or four inches taller than Cora and was dressed in a plaid shirt and a pair of jeans. There was a wholesome look in his eyes that seemed to glow in the presence of his wife. Emile saw the contentment and happiness that the couple shared. He was studying the portrait when Cora came out of her dressing room.

"That picture was taken just before we took him to the hospital. His condition continued to deteriorate from that moment to the end," she explained in a firm voice.

She was dressed in a dark blue dress with a white lace about her neck. The moment she entered the room he could feel her presence. She was beautiful even with her sad eyes. "How her husband must have loved her!" Emile said to himself.

"This may be the last time I wear a dress for a while," she smiled. "I've been thinking about what has passed between us, Emile." She paused and continued in a serious tone, "I think it's time for some straight talk."

"If there was ever a time for honestly expressing our thoughts, it's now, Cora."

"Yes, our lives are filled with uncertainties beyond our control. What I'm trying to say and am saying it badly, is that I value our friendship very much and am flattered that it is reciprocated by you."

"Cora," he said standing up to face her, "I understand what you're trying to say. I feel the same way. Our relationship is too new to start making commitments to a future that, at the minimum, looks bleak. What I was hoping was that we could write to each other. I'd like that a lot. I must tell you that I'll worry about your safety. I know how close to the front some of the medical units operate."

Cora picked up a small purse anxious to change the heavy conversation and said, "We could go to a good restaurant beside the Kennebec River."

"That would be great," he replied.

Chapter Twelve

Two days after his visit to see Cora Lambert, Emile was quietly reading the Sunday paper when his doorbell rang. It was a Western Union representative with a telegram. He thanked the man and closed the door, quite certain that it was the orders he expected.

To Lieutenant Colonel Emile Ranta:

You are ordered to report for duty September 30, 1941 to the commanding officer at Fort Benning Infantry School, Georgia.

General Nolan Hughes,

USA

His first thought was that it was great that he did not have to be there in the heat of summer, which could be almost unbearable to northerners like himself. He knew that his first duty was to train recruits for the potential task ahead. Emile cringed at the prospect of fighting on two different fronts. He knew how woefully unprepared the country was to implement such a thing without ample manpower or supplies. It wasn't going to be easy or quick, but Emile knew that the conversion to wartime goods was well underway. They just needed time, and he prayed that the good Lord would grant them that precious time before the homeland was invaded.

Faye had gone to her mother's that weekend to get more of the things she had left behind. He suspected that Bonnie's husband might have already been called and would not be at home. He reached for the phone and called her.

"Hello, Bonnie, this is Emile."

"I can't believe what has happened to us. Lewis has already been called to active duty," she cried in a loud voice.

"Yes, I'm not surprised. I've also been called to report in a few days to Benning. I wanted to say good-bye to Faye. I understood that she was with you this weekend. This is a bad time, Bonnie. No one knows what the future holds for us. We've got a lot of hard work ahead, that's for sure."

"I'll call Faye down, she's upstairs," Bonnie told him, screaming for Faye. "You know, Emile, a lot of bitterness has passed between us, and I apologize for all the grief I've caused you to bear. If I had it to live over again, I'd handle things differently. I hope I've matured into a better person. I want you to know that I don't hate you; we simply had differences that pulled us apart. You'll always be in my prayers, Em."

"Thanks for telling me that, Bonnie. The past is behind us, and we can't change what took place. I accept your apology. Right now I'm concerned about Alpha."

"It's frightening to think what this war will cost us," Bonnie replied with a tremulous voice. "You take care, Em. Here's Faye."

"Hi, Dad," Faye greeted him with a serious tone. "I was going to call you. I'll bet your battalion has already been activated. A friend of mine in the Army ROTC program at school warned me that units like yours are the first to be called to full duty. Your kindness and love will always be with me. Alpha and I have had the best Dad possible, and my love and prayers will follow you wherever you go. You haven't left home, and I'm already filled with worry."

"I wanted to say so-long for now. The battalion has been activated, but I'm not going with it. I'm ordered to the training depot at Benning. Well, sweetheart, your old dad will take care of himself; don't worry for me. My career as a soldier has prepared me for the fight that's heading for us. As soon as I can I'll write to let you know what my address is. Your letters will be the highlight of my day, regardless of where I am. I love you dearly, my precious daughter. Until next time, Honey."

"Good-bye, Dad, I love you."

Emile ran upstairs to pack his duffel bag. His conversation with Bonnie stayed with him for a long time. Her parting words had been sincere. The day she asked for a divorce was the worst day of his life, yet he had been able to accept the reality. They should never have married. One positive thing was the fact that he was able to be a father to their beloved Faye. She and Alpha had made his life meaningful, in contrast to their mother who had selfishly demanded whatever suited her, regardless of who it hurt. Since then, he had been able to live with the change without bitterness. He was thankful that he and Bonnie had been able to communicate amicably about the children. Other than that, he severed contact with her and concentrated on his own life without bitterness or rancor.

He had been thinking about Cora, and after he had packed, he sat down in the living room to call her.

She answered the phone. "Hello."

"Cora, this is Emile. I just received my orders and am leaving for Fort Benning today. I wanted to tell you how special the short time we've spent together has been to me. My life has had more meaning since you became a part of it. You've brought hope and happiness to a lonely person who went through each day without any promise that it would be any different from yesterday. Then you came along with your cute Chevrolet coupe, bringing sunshine where there was often darkness.

"Thank you, dear lady. Your gentle softness has enriched my life. I know that the future is filled with great uncertainties. I can accept whatever the future holds for me because I'm a soldier, and I'm prepared to do my duty. Knowing that I have your prayers and support will make it easier."

"Oh, Emile," she sighed. "I've been expecting this call. The future also frightens me. You're not the only one to be touched by our accidental meeting beside the Kennebec River. These are not normal times for us or for the country. I share your thoughts, Emile. Normally it would be prudent to be cautious and that we need more time... Having said that, I want you to know that I'll pray for you until we meet again. It's times like this that words fail me, dear friend. I'll write as often as I can when you send me your address. I'm also expecting orders any day now. Thanks for giving me some nice memories. I feel the same as you that our short time together has been special. May God watch over you, Emile. Until we meet again."

"Saying good-bye is harder than I anticipated, Cora."

"Why don't we just say 'so-long'?"

"Yes, until next time, Cora..." He hung up quickly. Their conversation had generated tears he could not control.

Emile took a train to Boston and boarded an Army plane directly to Fort Benning. Once he arrived there, he quickly became involved with the training of troops for the daunting task ahead of the country. The tempo increased each day reflecting the anxiety among the military personnel who knew just how badly they were prepared for the defense of the United States. He knew that Alpha was going to basic training at Fort Campbell, Kentucky.

The task of his training command was to turn young men barely out of high school into soldiers capable of defeating well-trained, superbly equipped, and highly-motivated enemy soldiers on the field of battle. There was no quick or easy way that could be accomplished. The recruits were coming out of a crippling depression that adversely affected every American family. Jobs were hard to come by, and most of the men were eager to accept the rigorous training routines because they had three meals a day and a clean bunk to sleep in.

Most of the men were already disciplined to accept hardships and demanding physical effort the long depression had forced upon them. That helped to condition them for that day when they meet the enemy in a life and death contest. Every day Emile stressed that training had to be as difficult as combat, and he demanded maximum effort from every recruit and every officer who had the grave responsibility of leading them into combat. He drove himself as hard as he did the men. When they had completed their recruit training ordeal, they were replaced by raw recruits, and the routines were implemented again.

Normally there would be some relief on Sundays, but these were not normal times. Troops were encouraged to attend church services, but their training routines continued immediately after services. Emile had regularly attended them once he arrived in Benning. On December 7, 1941, he had returned to his quarters to change into fatigues for a long march with full packs that had been scheduled. Just as he started out the door the executive officer of the training command met him at the door.

"Colonel," he explained, breathing heavily to catch his breath, "My God, Colonel Ranta, the Japanese have attacked us at Pearl Harbor!"

Emile heard what the Captain was telling him, and he felt sick to his stomach. His first thought was for Alpha. "Captain, cancel today's march. Tell the troops to return to barracks and to turn their radios on. Can you take me to headquarters?"

"Sure, Colonel. I've got the company Jeep," he replied.

The news on the radio had significantly changed everything. The country was now at war against Japan. There was a silent pause of reflection in the headquarters operations room. Those individuals who knew how unprepared the nation was to fight the Asian aggressor were deeply concerned. Senior officers were mentally setting priorities for the immediate future of their commands. The only ray of hope that Sunday morning was the long distance that separated Japan from the United States mainland. The only exception was Alaska. The Aleutian Islands pointed like a dagger to the mainland and were within striking distance of the Japanese Islands. Alaska was even less prepared to defend against a determined attack than the lower forty-eight states.

Every officer on the base was called into a conference. It was a sober gathering of men who would have the herculean task of defending the nation. The General got up from his desk and walked to a large map on the wall of the Aleutian Islands.

"There's a real possibility that Japan may attack us here. They could land troops and occupy the islands with only a token resistance from our troops in the area. At the present we're unable to adequately supply those troops stationed on some of the larger islands in the string. That also goes for our air power. I've just been ordered to send more men and equipment into Alaska via British Columbia. Our Canadian friends are as unprepared as we are, but our effort in Alaska will be a joint operation. Both nations can assemble a more formidable force than either country is capable of at this crucial point of time."

Emile had listened to the General and raised his hand to speak. "I understand that every move we now make is an effort to buy time until we're ready to confront such a determined enemy. I've been following the war in Europe very closely, General, and I'm convinced that they, too, will declare war upon us at this time of crisis."

"I think we all agree with that assessment, Colonel Ranta. What do you propose that we do about it beside tread water and bide our time until we are better prepared to take on two powerful enemies?"

"I don't have any magic wand, Sir, but I've been fascinated by the creation in England of small units of well-trained commandoes capable of making fast hit-and-run operations along the North Atlantic coast. England's hope is that the raids will cause Germany to send more troops to those more vulnerable locations. That kind of strategy leaves fewer troops available to cross the English Channel and attack England proper. What I'm trying to say, Sir, is that we should consider the formation of small well-trained light infantry units much like Roger's Rangers in the French and Indian War in the early 1700's."

"I like your suggestion, Colonel. However, we have a more urgent need to train more troops for defense of the homeland." The General looked around the room with a determined look and said, "This is not a planning meeting, men. I simply wanted to impress upon you the urgency of accelerating our training agenda, Return to your commands and be prepared for the influx of recruits that are on their way to this facility. Colonel Ranta, I want to speak to you in private."

"Yes, Sir," Emile replied, hoping that he had not been too critical at a very difficult time. He waited for the room to empty.

"Come into my private office where we can talk freely, Colonel." General Holmes pointed to a room beside the conference hall. "Please have a seat. You may smoke if you wish."

"I'm not a habitual smoker, Sir. I occasionally smoke a pipe when I'm in the woods." Emile took a seat in front of the General's desk.

"Your comments about light infantry interest me. I agree with you that we'll need specially trained troops to perform jobs very similar to those of the famous Rangers. The Army staff believes that Germany will be a greater threat to our safety than Japan." The General looked at a large map of the world on his wall and continued in a serious tone. "England is on the verge of collapse. German submarines are sinking more shipping destined to the British Isles than is being built in England or the United States combined."

"My God!" Emile exclaimed.

"Yes, Colonel, I tell you this because we need to do everything possible to keep England free of invasion by the very able German Army. The bombing of England's cities, airfields, military installations, and industrial capacity is taking place on a daily basis. Time is running out!"

"I agree, Sir."

"Now, Colonel Ranta, you must swear to secrecy what I'm about to tell you. Understood?"

"Understood, Sir," Emile replied, anxious to hear what the General had to say.

"My dear friend, Colonel Lucien Truscott, has already been dispatched to England to study the possibility of forming commando-like U.S. troops. The British Commandoes are the best trained and most tenacious fighters in Great Britain. Truscott has already recommended that we form similar units. The Ranger title has already been suggested by the Army Staff."

"I'm encouraged to hear that, General."

The General smiled and made eye contact with Emile. "Now I'm asking you to volunteer for the task of organizing and training the first battalion of Rangers. That means you would have to put your personal affairs in order prior to being shipped to Scotland. What do you say, Colonel?"

"I'd be honored to accept the challenge, Sir. By the way where are we going to get the men?

"I assumed that you'd accept the offer. Your Maine National Guard unit has already been activated. You may pick potential lieutenant platoon leaders and enlisted sergeants from their ranks to form a nucleus for the balance of the battalion which may be selected from those troops already in Ireland and the British Isles," the General replied.

"I understand that time is crucial, but how much time do I have to pick my core components before flying to Scotland?"

"You may return to your normal training command tomorrow morning and turn it over to your staff. You will have five days to say good-bye to your family and friends. However, you must submit the names of the men who will accompany you to Scotland by noon tomorrow. You'll report to Fort Devens in Massachusetts in five days for your transportation orders. I wish you God speed, Colonel."

"I appreciate your confidence in me, General," Emile saluted and left his office, thrilled that he was selected for such a demanding task.

Chapter Thirteen

Emile quickly selected several officers from the training command at Benning and the rest from his Sanford infantry unit which was located at Fort Stewart, Georgia. He was anxious to review the roster of the unit once he arrived at Fort Stewart. Most Maine men had already been hardened by the vicious depression that had spread all across the nation for years prior to December 7th. He was certain that his Maine soldiers could meet the demanding requirements of a Ranger battalion. He planned to use them as a vital core around which he would select more men once he was in Scotland. This was his first step in forming a special operations unit that traditionally was assigned to dangerous missions behind enemy lines and against superior numbers of enemy forces. He silently prayed for the ability to perform such a demanding task.

On his last day at Benning, he received a letter from Cora telling him that her medical company had been activated and sent to Fort Stewart. He was pleased and looked forward to seeing her before he was shipped out to Scotland via Fort Devens.

England was under siege. German planes were launching raids on a daily basis against London and other targets. By 1942, France, Yugoslavia, Italy, Belgium, Finland, Norway, and all of Europe was in flames. Germany's massive armies of men, planes and tanks   controlled every nation except England and those who remained neutral. Fear gripped the world. The only hope of the civilized world was resting on the United States who was desperately preparing for the brutal war ahead of them. There was an air of apprehension when the American public checked their daily papers in the morning.

Emile went to Fort Stewart training depot heavily burdened by the unprecedented demand placed on his shoulders. Yet, the sneak attack at Pearl Harbor had ignited a determined hatred against the Japanese and the Germans that inspired the industrial might of the nation to collectively roll up their sleeves. Every industry in the country was in the process of converting to produce military goods and supplies on a scale never experienced. All they needed was a little bit of time, and they would force the aggressors to pay a heavy price for their brutal attack against neighboring nations.

Emile went immediately to the base headquarters to determine the status of the men he had selected from his National Guard unit. The Executive Officer at the base told him that they were being processed as they spoke. "You'll be pleased, Colonel Ranta. The men you selected have been relieved of their current commands and have been placed in barracks for immediate shipping orders. They've already drawn full field uniforms and been issued the new Garand M-1 rifle and a few Thompson submachine guns.

"I could not be more pleased," Emile said, smiling. "All we have to do now is wait for transportation. Are we going to Scotland by ship or by plane?"

"Our orders from Benning were specific. You're going by plane, Colonel Ranta. You'll leave Georgia by rail to Boston or to Bangor, Maine, in two days. You're checked in at the Stewart hospitality center for the two nights you'll be here."

"I'm impressed by your efficiency," Emile replied.

"These are trying times that require extraordinary efforts, Colonel. We're in the process of breaking up all of the National Guard units into smaller components around which we'll develop more platoons and companies."

"They're good men, General. It was a privilege to command them," he replied. "By the way, I have a friend in a medical company from Maine that was ordered to Fort Stewart. Have they arrived yet, General?"

The General scanned some papers on his desk and said, "Yes, they've already occupied quarters here near the base headquarters. You'll find them right around the corner from the entrance, Colonel."

"Thank you, Sir," Emile replied and saluted, anxious to see if Cora was on base. He located the quarters for the company and saw Cora sitting at a desk packing small bottles in a cardboard box. She was turned away from the entrance and did not see him. He smiled seeing how intense she was checking the medicine bottles against a long list on her desk. She had her hair pulled back of her ears, fastened with two red barrettes.

"Hello, stranger," he greeted her.

She turned her head, dropping the bottle she had in her hand. "Emile, you surprised me!" she exclaimed, getting out of her chair.

He held out his arms to her, and she came into his embrace. "I was hoping I'd have a chance to see you, Cora. Would you be able to see me at the Officers' Club tonight?"

She left his embrace and picked up the aspirin bottle on the floor. "Maybe I could swap my duty at the dispensary tonight with a friend. Let me call the desk. How long are you going to be here, Emile?"

"I don't have much time. I'll be leaving in the morning," he replied with an anxious look on his face.

"Can you tell me where you're going?"

"I can't tell you, Cora."

"I understand," she said, picking up the phone. "Things are happening at a rapid pace. We're getting ready to join a division staging center… I'm calling to see if I can swap schedules with someone."

He saw the look on her face when her superior approved her request.

"That was my company commander. He gave me a pass for the rest of the day and until tomorrow morning, provided I finish packing this box of aspirin. Would you mind if I stopped at my quarters to change into something besides these fatigue coveralls?"

He was pleased with her response. "I'll take you any way I can get you," he grinned. "I have a Jeep outside for as long as I need it. Rank has its privileges… I'd be honored to drop you off at your quarters and wait for you."

"You've made my day, Emile," she replied, touching his arm.

While he was waiting for Cora to change, he sat in the Jeep and wrote a note to Faye at the University of New Hampshire and to Alpha who was at Fort Dix. He had just sealed the envelopes when she came out of the barracks building. She was dressed in the regulation Army uniform of the day.

"The uniform is becoming to you, Cora," he said, jumping out to assist her into the passenger seat of the Jeep.

"I was thinking the same thing about you, Colonel. My friends are envious," she smiled.

The officers' club was filled to capacity. "I've never seen it so crowded. There's a seat in the quiet area at the far end of the ballroom. Let's grab it while we can."

Leaving their caps on the empty table, they went to the large cafeteria-style serving area. Emile thought that it might be a long time that he wouldn't be able to have a tender, juicy steak, so he selected a medium rare one with mash potatoes. Cora selected macaroni and cheese, green beans, and a salad. They both had coffee.

Emile thought that Cora was a little more reserved than usual. He told her about Alpha and Faye who had one more semester and she would then get her teaching certificate. They ate in silence until Emile announced that he wanted a refill of coffee. "Can I get something for you, Cora?"

She replied in a soft voice, "I would like a hot cup of tea. I don't have room for a dessert."

"I think I'll look over the pie situation. If they have a custard pie, I'll get one," he grinned and left.

When he returned to their table with a tray of tea, coffee, and pie he saw Cora turn away from him to hide the tears that were in her eyes. He placed the cup of tea in front of her and grasped her hands in his. "What's wrong, Cora?"

She squeezed his hands and quickly withdrew hers to take a handkerchief from her purse, wiping her eyes. "I wanted so much to make this a pleasant evening so that we'd have pleasant memories of the occasion when are far apart in a world that's tearing itself to pieces. I'm so sorry, Emile, to carry on this way. To be honest, I'm frightened. Ever since we left Maine, I can't get those images of broken bodies out of my mind. The war has just started, and I can't get it out of my mind. I'm overwhelmed by its capacity to destroy lives and wonder if I have the courage to handle the bleak reality..."

"Dear lady." Emile was a witness to her most inner feelings, and in that moment he realized that he had fallen in love with this gracious lady. "I don't have any answers, Cora. I've spent most of my adult life in the Army. Defending our way of life has become a normal part of who I am. I understand what you're saying. If I was to tell you that the road ahead of us was going to be easy, it would be a lie. It's going to be hard on all of us, especially nurses like you who have the impossible job of mending broken bodies and minds. I've found that knowing that someone cares for us and prays for our safety helps to sustain those who are on the front lines."

Cora looked into his eyes and quickly added: "I know that my work as a nurse is important. To be honest I'm not worried for my own safety. I'm worried for you, dear friend."

They were two people representative of the nation that was desperately preparing for a war against two powerful opponents on two different fronts with an Army that was not much more than a small constabulary force. When Cora finished her cup of tea and Emile took the last bite of his custard pie, Emile suggested that they take in the movie *Casablanca*, with Humphrey Bogart and Ingrid Bergmann at the base theatre.

"That sounds like a good idea," Cora answered. "It's been a long time since I went to the movies. Going alone made me feel even more alone, so I avoided them. Thanks for suggesting it," she added, walking out of the Officers' Club on Emile's arm. She had not been at a movie since her husband passed away. She noted that Emile was quieter than usual.

He carried his responsibility with a quiet dignity that, at times did not invite idle chatter. As they drove to the base theatre in the Jeep, he wondered if there was ever going to be a tomorrow for him and Cora. He parked the Jeep and turned to her. "Cora, I know that what I'm going to say may be too bold in these troubled times of uncertainty, but it's important for me to tell you that you've become an important part of my life. Perhaps I'm asking for too much in the short duration of our relationship. Will you wait for me and write when you can? I promise to do the same...

It was too dark for them to look into each other's eyes. She took his hands in hers and kissed them. "I'm honored to be the object of your affections, Emile," she replied in a soft voice. "You've read my mind. I've been thinking the same thing, and I'm not handling the fact that the future is in question... Yes, I'll be waiting for you. You've been in my prayers since we first met, but we do need more time to grow the relationship. That will give us something to dream about and look forward to," she replied, getting out of the Jeep. "For tonight, let's enjoy the show."

Two hours later, they exited the theatre. Cora was dressed in her regular uniform jacket. It was cooler than usual for Georgia. Emile had left an Army overcoat in the back seat, and he reached for it. "This will keep you warmer for the ride back to your quarters, Cora."

"It does feel good," she answered. "Thanks for suggesting a movie. It was a sad and sobering ending appropriate for the mood that permeates this Army base."

Emile stopped the Jeep at a street lamp in front of Cora's barracks. Turning off the engine, he held out his hand to her holding a small satin box. "I hope that you will accept this, dear lady."

She took the case and opened it. Inside was a simple engagement ring. The light from the lamp was bright enough for her to read the note accompanying it:

"Until we meet again, this ring is a symbol of my love and devotion and commitment to a future with you."

"Emile!" she exclaimed, "I do accept it, thank you. It will make the days we're apart more endurable. Thank you for being the kind, caring person you are. This has been quite an evening. I promise to write as often as I can, Emile."

They warmly embraced and kissed beneath the light of the lamppost. "Until next time, Cora," Emile came around the Jeep to help her get out of the vehicle.

"Until next time, Emile," she answered in a faltering voice. She opened the door and turned to him with glistening eyes. "You be careful, wherever you're going, Soldier."

Emile nodded his head and climbed into the Jeep. She had seen tears in his eyes too…

Chapter Fourteen

Later that same evening, Emile was sitting in a lawn chair inside of a DC3 transport plane loaded with field rations and food supplies destined for an air base in Northern Ireland. He was the only passenger. Immediately after saying good-bye to Cora he had returned to his quarters at the base hospitality center. New orders were waiting for him with a train ticket to Manchester, New Hampshire, where he was ordered to board the transport plane at Grenier Field. He had rushed to catch the train carrying a small duffel bag for his personal belongings, disappointed that he did not have a chance to call Cora one last time.

The lumbering transport plane did not have any windows in the cargo compartment. That made it impossible for him to read or write a letter to Faye and Alpha, so he laid his head against the chair and closed his eyes. He was weary, yet, he could not sleep. His head was filled with thoughts about the monumental task ahead of him. He questioned his ability to accomplish what was expected of him in the short time available, and with the limited source of manpower and equipment in the British Isles.

The German army was rolling through and occupying Greece, Yugoslavia, Belgium, France, and Denmark with little or no resistance. Japan was also forcing their will into the Pacific by occupying all of the islands from the Philippines to New Guinea, creating a serious threat to Australia and New Zealand. Two powerful and ruthless armies were victorious wherever they proposed to attack. The world scene looked grim. Those men, like Emile, who were responsible for the undertaking to stop their advance against the rest of the world were amazed at the weak resistance of the French to the Germans. France had outnumbered the Germans in tanks and men, yet they yielded to the rapid blitzkrieg of the Germans. Their capitulation left the British Isles most vulnerable to an amphibious invasion by the resourceful German high command. England simply did not have the resources to repel such an attack in the early months of 1942.

The United State, Canada, and England were desperately working to maintain a steady supply line across the North Atlantic Ocean to keep England in the war while they all worked miracles to increase their industrial conversion from civilian to military products. The German submarines were sinking more transports in the North Atlantic than the three countries were capable of producing.

Emile was aware of the situation, and that frightened him more than anything else. He was also informed of the successful creation of the British Commandoes and their daring amphibious attacks with small numbers of men at German occupied installations along the eastern coast of Europe. They had already won the respect of military men all over the world by creating a potential threat to any German stronghold with their rapid hit-and-run tactics. Emile intended to create an American force with the same capabilities as the Commandoes. He intended to use the same tactical techniques and training camps. As a matter of a fact, he was urged to have the American troops train with the British. That idea appealed to him. He knew that the Commandoes had eagerly adopted the American built Thompson submachine. It was light, easy to use and had a deadly rate of fire. It was the ultimate weapon for rapid hit-and-run raids where a small force inflicted maximum damage to an enemy installation. If that tactic was repeated often enough, the enemy would have to increase their manpower wherever they were threatened. Thus, that increase of manpower by the enemy decreased the potential of German attack against England. The raids were a means of buying time for the formidable ability of the United States industrial might to work their miracle.

The cadre of young men he had selected from his National Guard units to help him train the special force were the best men he had ever served with. Their availability made the task ahead easier. Every leader of men in combat soon recognizes that unit cohesion is a must ingredient in any formation of soldiers. That is the mark of good leadership and spells success or failure of the unit to carry out its missions. Emile knew that respect for the men started with him and worked its way down the chain of command. Once the men recognize that their commander is interested in their welfare and has respect for them, the men quickly respond in a positive fashion. Respect comes from the top down, and not every commander has learned that basic tenet of command. Emile intended to start the training sessions by implementing the old Army buddy system and raising it to a higher level. Individual initiative would be encouraged and rewarded. He was just as anxious to start the training sessions as the higher command was for him to implement it.

Ever since Emile had been handed the job, he thought about the very successful Rogers' Rangers who served valiantly during the French and Indian Wars. It was his intention to create a similar body of men capable of successfully handling any mission assigned to them. Being able to function in small groups behind enemy lines without support elements would be a specialty. Along these lines he also planned to introduce Rogers' twenty-seven Rules of Ranging. They outlined acceptable conduct during attacks on enemy installations; conduct on the trail; and basic infantry "fire and movement" tactics.

Emile had jotted down on his pocket booklet six creeds that he intended to instill in every recruit:

1. I am an American Soldier.
2. I am a guardian of freedom and the American way of life.
3. I will always place the mission first.
4. I will never accept defeat.
5. I will never quit.
6. I will never leave a fallen comrade.

Emile hoped to develop a small mobile force of well-trained men capable of carrying out missions behind enemy lines; against coastal installations; gathering of intelligence whenever and wherever it was needed; and scouting in advance of attacking units. The newly trained force would be ideal for the hit-and-run raids such as the Commandoes had so successfully done. A General Eisenhower on the Army staff in Washington had suggested that the men Emile was ordered to train be called Army Rangers after the famed Rogers' Rangers. Emile had told his superiors that he was very much in favor of the name, but so far it had not been officially announced. He was a student of early American history and was an admirer of General John Stark who had performed heroic feats as an officer in Rogers' Rangers during the French and Indian Wars and also served with distinction during the Revolutionary War. His brilliant victory at the Battle of Bennington, Vermont, in 1777 had set the stage for the defeat of General Burgoyne at Saratoga. Emile especially admired Stark for his audacity and skills in leading irregular troops against the enemies of the country, and once the guns were silent, he retired to his farm in New Hampshire, a true Cincinnatus.

The plane landed at a small airfield in Northern Ireland where Emile was greeted by an American Colonel in charge of an infantry regiment stationed near the coast a few miles north of Dublin.

"I'm Colonel Knowles, and have been ordered to assist you in anyway possible, Colonel Ranta," Knowles saluted him.

Emile returned his salute and surveyed the airfield. "It feels good to stretch my legs, Colonel."

"I'll escort you to your quarters. I understand that you'll be selecting men from my regiment and from several small Army detachments in the British Isles. I've been ordered to supply you with anything you'll need, especially clothing, weapons and munitions. You are lucky, Colonel. We have just received a fresh supply of Thompson submachine guns and ammunition. The British Commandoes have adopted it as their preferred weapon," Colonel Knowles smiled.

Emile appraised the young, slender Colonel Knowles as several years younger than he was. "My name is Emile, Colonel. Why not call each other by our first names?"

"It's my pleasure, Emile. My name is Hector, but most of the officers here in Northern Ireland call me Slim."

"Then Slim it is." Emile grabbed his duffel bag and followed Slim to a waiting Dodge command car.

There were two full divisions of American troops already in Northern Ireland. Emile had the authority to requisition men, equipment, and supplies he needed to train and equip his special forces. "I know that I'm going to call on your limited resources, Slim, and I apologize for that. The first item on my long list of things to-do is selection of two companies of men. I hope you and your fellow officers in the two divisions here are not opposed to thinning your ranks of some of your best men."

"We've been expecting that, Emile. As a matter of fact, I've already selected a few members of my artillery battalion. They're from a National Guard unit in North Dakota and I've been impressed with their discipline and competence," Slim told him.

"When I left the regular Army I joined a New Hampshire National Guard back home. They lacked a lot of materials and equipment but they made up for it with ingenuity and good old-fashioned common sense. I expect all of the reserves will give a good accounting of themselves. My orders are to select and train a battalion of men in as short a time as possible. Time is of the essence, Slim."

"I gathered that by the orders we received to assist you in that task. I'll show you the officers' quarters and an office set up for your command. The Officers' Club is to our right, and the enlisted mess hall is next to it." Slim pointed to the two Quonset hut structures.

"This is one area where we part from normal protocol," Emile quickly informed him. "Officers and enlisted men are to share the same barracks and the same mess facilities. We'll work with the men at all times and share the same training exercises without exception. That includes me, too."

"There is a British Commando officer here anxious to meet you. He's the one who will train your battalion their initial specialist training along with his Commandoes. Most of your training will take place in Achnacarry, Scotland, home to the British Commando Training Depot, across the North Channel," Slim said.

For the next few days, Emile worked long hours interviewing every man he had selected after checking their records. Those men he had selected from his Maine National

Guard had arrived, relieving him of the many duties that had limited his time interviewing the men he would lead into combat. It was important to him that he evaluate their past performance, and he wanted to   look into each man's eyes when he was told the truth about the grave risks and grueling training ordeal he would have to endure. He also emphasized that the missions he would be ordered to carry out were infinitely more dangerous than anything he would encounter in a conventional infantry regiment. Only a select few would earn the privilege of belonging to the best trained battalion in the United States Army. Many would be called; few would be accepted.

The initial specialist training for the first cadre of troops was conducted with the assistance of an experienced British Commando officer. He had outlined that all men, officers and enlisted men, would go through a three-day exercise which consisted of the following routines:

1. Speed marches of three to sixteen miles each with obstacle courses along the way to build body strength and stamina.

2. Training with various weapons; including British, American, and German appropriate for light infantry use.

3. Learning tactical skills, scouting, patrolling, silent killing of enemy subjects, mountain climbing, river crossing, and street fighting.

Nine days later, they had successfully completed the above three exercises and were immediately transferred to the west coast of Scotland to the famous British Commando training depot at Achnacarry Castle. The battalion was beginning to take shape. Thirty percent of the original men had failed to meet the high standards established for the battalion, and were sent back to their original units. Ten percent had voluntarily dropped out the first week. Emile was probably having more physical aches and pains than the younger men. He was feeling his age, but had endured the ordeal and won the respect of the younger men. His original orders that officers did not have special privileges were understood by all concerned, even though the men doubted it at first. These simple elements of command added to his interpretation of unit cohesion, and he was pleased to witness that it was working. They had bonded as a unit and fully accepted him as an equal. He was proud of the men, and they knew that his feelings were sincere.

While they were training in Scotland, Germany successfully occupied France. The surviving British and French forces had been evacuated at Dunkirk. It was a sad day for England. She now stood alone and vulnerable to an invasion that she was ill-prepared to repulse. It was this vulnerability that urged England to expand its Commando operations so as to keep the German troops along the French coast on the defensive instead of preparing for an invasion across the English Channel.

Training exercises for the American troops were stepped up as they worked along beside their English brothers. The drills trained the men in amphibious assaults of beaches and fortified installations. Other skills taught included navigation, cliff assaults, silent night operations against an inland enemy position, and taking of prisoners.

In the third week in June, Emile called the battalion together. They assembled at the parade field in front of the British Commando Headquarters. "Men," he announced with a smile on his face, "today, I have the privilege to announce that we are officially designated as the First Ranger Battalion of the United States Army. Congratulations."

The men responded with a loud "yo!"

"I'm proud of all of you and will give you my best. Platoon commanders have the new Ranger shoulder patches for distribution. You are going to be free of training exercises for the next few days while we distribute new weapons and field gear. Enjoy your short respite from drills. I also want to caution you against writing home about what we're doing here. So far we have remained a secret force. When we do carry the fight to the enemy they will know who we are."

The men erupted in a loud and shrill "yes!...yes!...."

Emile dismissed the battalion and turned to his British counterpart, Colonel John Earhart. "What's next, John?"

"We're contemplating an assault against a German installation on the French coast. If we're ever to reverse the advances of the Germans, we've got develop tactics and

106

strategies that work against heavily fortified coast strongholds using air, naval and amphibious forces all coordinated to function as a whole. It will be a difficult invasion at best, so we've got to begin assaults on a small basis so that we can develop techniques to coordinate these larger forces. Keep this information to yourself. Churchill has ordered us to take direct action against German occupied Europe. He described the Commando raids with these words:"

"There comes out from the sea from time to time a hand of steel that plucks German sentries from their posts with growing efficiency."

"I'm proud to invite our Ranger brothers on our next raid which I believe is Dieppe," John enthusiastically announced.

"We're ready to be a part of the Prime Minister's 'hand of steel.' I'll be looking forward to serving with you, John."

Chapter Fifteen

Emile stepped up the rigorous training schedule for the battalion when he was informed that portions of the battalion would participate in an assault on Fortress Europe. It was called *Operation Jubilee* and was designed to test the strength of the German defenses on the northern coast of France, which would give the Allies some measure of the possibility of seizing a workable port of entry into France and Germany. It was also an opportunity to evaluate the coordination of land, sea, and air military components. Most of the troops were Canadian Army. A small number of Rangers and Commandoes were used.

The port selected for the assault was Dieppe on the French coast, 60 kilometers south of the Belgium border. Several large German batteries were positioned strategically to cover any angle of approach to the coast line. Emile and his Rangers were assigned to a British Commando unit with the task of eliminating one of the large caliber coastal artillery installations. Most of them were armed with a Thompson submachine gun or the M-1 Garand rifle.

Prior to the attack, Emile had the battalion go through live-fire-fire training exercises. They were also introduced to the infamous British Commando twenty-foot elevated jumping platform in Scotland with full packs and weapons. It was the most difficult and demanding training exercise the Rangers experienced so far. Emile made the jump with his men without any injuries, but it rattled his head inside the helmet he was wearing. The Ranger behind him suffered serious back injuries and several sprained their ankles.

There was some disappointment within the ranks when Emile informed the men that they had orders for the Dieppe amphibious raid. Only forty four men and five officers were assigned to the Canadian division. There were a few British, Polish, and French troops also assigned to the Canadians. The Rangers were moved to the North Sea for amphibious training by the Royal Navy. Other skills such as navigation and cliff assaults on coastal batteries were a part of their three-day training schedule.

The day of the assault on Dieppe, a vast armada of warships was assembled in the English Channel. The Rangers joined a company of British Commandos in slow-moving wooden landing craft known as "Eureka's," with specific orders to neutralize a German artillery battery. Once the operation got under way, several of the small craft developed engine trouble and were left behind. It was not a good omen for a successful operation. About seven miles from the target area, the craft with Emile and most of his men ran into a German Naval patrol. An intense fire-fight developed that sank several of the landing craft and dispersed the rest. The only boats to reach the designated target area included the one that contained Emile and his men.

The master plan for the operation called for the boats to reach the target under the cover of darkness. Delays en route caused the men to come ashore in broad daylight. They were soon pinned down by heavy enemy fire from machine guns and heavy caliber cannons that killed several American Rangers and British Commandoes before they landed on the beach. Total confusion developed at or near the beaches where heavy losses were absorbed by the attackers. The time tables that planners had spent hours to develop was in total disarray.

The sheer firepower of the German batteries was overwhelming. The only successful effort was carried out by a British Commando unit accompanied by several American Rangers with Emile in command. They hit the German batteries with great speed and surprise which overwhelmed the defenders, but it was a hollow victory. The Dieppe raid was a disaster that cost the lives of seventy percent of the attackers. Thirty-four hundred men were lost. Emile was slightly wounded by a piece of shrapnel in his left leg. Seven Rangers were killed or taken prisoner, seven men were wounded. Four American officers and thirty-nine men survived the failed assault. Most of the losses were absorbed by the gallant Canadians.

The Allies had suffered losses, but they had gained valuable experience. Training efforts reflected that experience. One of the main lessons learned at Dieppe was that coastal Europe could more readily be invaded from beaches instead of through entrenched fortified ports. This lesson was successfully applied when fortress Europe was invaded over the beaches of Normandy, June 6, 1944.

Emile had adamantly refused to be hospitalized with his wounds. He was able to move about with a cane and wanted to accompany his battalion so that they could complete their training in Scotland.

When they arrived in Scotland, Emile was anxious to check for letters from home. He returned to his quarters and opened one from Cora.

August 1, 1942

Dear Emile,

Tonight, I'm filled with apprehension that this war is turning out to be more costly in human lives than I ever anticipated. It seems that the Germans and the Japanese are able to invade countries, readily brushing aside any resistance from the Allies. I pray often for your safety, Emile.

I've just completed a thorough refresher course in the treatment of wounded men that will be helpful to those nurses who attended. We are getting ready for shipment to the Pacific coast, so we can assume that we'll be assigned to the Pacific area.

I think often of you and recall with a smile of how fortunate that you and your son were available to fix the flat tire on my Chevrolet coupe.

I haven't heard from you, so I assume that you are busy training troops. There's a full moon out tonight. I hope it is shining on you. May God keep you safe, Emile.

All my best,
Cora Lambert

Emile placed the letter on his field desk and sat down to change the bandage on his left leg. He had a letter from Alpha, Faye, and Bonnie. Alpha was in the last period of his training exercises and seemed comfortable with his decision to join instead of waiting to be drafted. His closest buddy was a Swedish boy from Monson, Maine. Emile smiled remembering how easy it was to bond with men experiencing the same things in their unit. It was called "unit cohesion" and was the heart and soul of a good Army combat organization. Buddies were important, especially in combat when your life depended on them. Alpha's letter was positive and brought a smile to his lips when he asked if he would have to salute his father when they met.

The letter from Faye was also cheerful. His two children had grown up and he was proud of them. Fay wrote:

Berlin, NH

September 1, 1942

Dear Dad,

Now that I've finished school, I'll be moving into the house. How lucky I was to get a job as a fourth-grade-teacher in Berlin. That way I can stay at home and take care of the place too.

I've had a couple of letters from Alpha. I think he's homesick, but he'll never admit it. I miss him. We were not only brother and sister growing up but, also, good friends. He has your gentle temperament, Dad.

The town is almost void of young men. Almost every male in my graduating class is in the armed forces. I pray for all of them as I do for you and Alpha. I hope that when this ugly war is over you will be able to find peace and contentment with someone who has won your heart. Alpha and I talked a lot about your new friend, Cora. We both wish you all the best, Dad. You've handled disappointments in your life with unbelievable grace and courage. We admire you for your strength and inherent decency.

Alpha and I love you, Dad. May the good Lord look after you and keep you safe.

Faye

Emile was interrupted by a courier who handed him a satchel with new orders. He placed it on his field desk and opened Bonnie's letter:

Burlington, Vt.

August 25, 1942

Dear Em,

I pray that this finds you doing well and not in combat. I just received a telegram from the Marine Corps that Lewis has been killed-in-action somewhere in the Pacific theatre. I've written to Alpha and Faye to give them the news.

Lewis and I did not have as good a marriage as you and I had. Perhaps I'm to blame more than either of you. I hope that I've grown up more…This telegram has shattered my world, and I don't know how I'm going to handle it. It was only natural to share my thoughts with you. You were always strong and handled adversity with unbelievable courage. I hope you don't mind.

Our daughter is so pleased to get the job in Berlin. She'll be good in the classroom. Alpha has grown into a nice young man. I hear from him often. He'll soon be finished with his basic training, and that fact is frightening to me.

I sincerely hope that this note finds you well, Emile. The brutal reality of this war has made it easier for me to better appreciate the dedication and commitment you have shown over the years serving this country. I did not always appreciate your strong sense of duty to a cause greater than yourself. Now, I realize how badly this country needs men like you.

I pray for your forgiveness, Em. Regardless of our differences, I want you to know that I've always been proud of you.

Stay safe, Em,

Bonnie

The dispatch pouch contained new orders for the Ranger battalion. They were now attached to the Army's First Division, the famous "Red One." His elite special Ranger force was going to link up with the best division in the Army. They were to be part of the amphibious operation against North Africa. Emile placed the letters and the pouch on the desk and stretched out on his cot. He was exhausted. He thought of his two children and how lucky he was to have them. His final thoughts were about Cora before fatigue shut his body and mind to rest.

The next morning he wrote a short note to Alpha and to Faye. He could not tell them where he was or what he was doing, all he could say was that he was getting along fine and that he missed them very much. He told Cora how she was often in his thoughts. He had already made up his mind that he loved her, yet it was too soon to declare such feelings. He wrote a reply to Bonnie.

Somewhere in Europe

Dear Bonnie,

Received your letter and am sorry about Lewis. As a career soldier, I know how difficult it is to lose a loved one on the battlefield, but that's different from those at home when they receive a telegram that shatters lives and leaves a helpless feeling. What does one say at such a tragic moment? I pray that you'll find strength to accept your loss, Bonnie. I'm sure that Lewis was a brave marine. Over the years I've had some differences with my marine brothers, but I never questioned their devotion and heroism in defending our country against its enemies.

You know how it is, Bonnie. I can't tell you where I am or what I'm doing. All I can say is that I'm doing my best, and sometimes that does not seem to be enough…

I pray that God will bring peace and comfort to you during this time of crisis. Try to be worthy of your husband's sacrifice.

All my best,
Emile

Chapter Sixteen

Operation Torch, the invasion of North Africa early in November, took place with Emile's battalion leading the amphibious troops in Morocco. The resistance by the Vichy French was strong in places, and at several locations French forces welcomed the Americans. Once the Americans got ashore, they met fierce resistance from the well-entrenched Germans. Losses were greater than anticipated. In one place, known as Kasserine Pass, the inexperienced American troops were pushed back fifty miles by Marshall Rommel's Tank-led offensive with extremely heavy losses. It was a bitter defeat for the green American troops.

Emile's battalion had been by-passed by the German troops once the Americans gave ground. Being the experienced combat officer that he was, Emile recognized that he was in a dangerous situation and had his men seize a prominent hill to the north towards the Mediterranean. The Germans had placed an artillery control unit on the hilltop. The Rangers took the location with light losses and dug deep foxholes so that they could defend the position. They had a panoramic view around them. His radio team was able to make contact with the retreating American forces and also with the U. S. Navy support ships just off the northern coast of Morocco.

While the Rangers were preparing the hilltop for a vigorous defense, the Germans surrounded them with heavy tanks. Whenever the tanks were a threat to their position, Emile called in the quadrants for Navy support. They were able to accurately keep the Germans from scaling the hill. Emile's quick decision to assault the prominence saved his battalion from annihilation. Their location was also defended by a new weapon called a "bazooka" that had been issued to the Rangers just prior to their shipping out from England. It had the capacity of a 75 mm cannon and was operated by a two-men crew. It was a long tube that launched a rocket capable of stopping a tank. It was a welcomed addition to the infantrymen. The Rangers had four of them. It was the ultimate armor-piercing weapon. The battalion, with some assistance from the Navy, was able to knock out most of the tanks that were threatening the hilltop.

The fight for the most prominent real estate for miles around was viciously contested by both sides. Gunfire filled the air, and the two-men bazooka teams challenged several of the attacking German tanks. Emile was wounded by shrapnel from an exploding German artillery shell while he was assisting one of the bazooka teams on the lip of the hill. The crew immediately called for a medic and continued to fire at the tanks while Emile's blood formed puddles in the desert sand.

Emile's executive officer, Major Saul Hopkins, took command of the battalion while a medic worked feverishly trying to stem the flow of blood from Emile's shattered body. While that was taking place, the Germans withdrew from the area when a column of American and British tanks had been speeding toward the hill to insure that it remained in the Allies' hands. Emile was placed in a stretcher and taken to the coast by a British tank where he was transferred to the large hospital ship off shore.

Ten days after the battle for the hilltop, Emile was in a ward aboard the hospital ship wrapped like a mummy. The left side of his body had been violated by small jagged pieces of hot steel. The leg had absorbed most of the force of the exploding shell filled with nail-like particles to inflict maximum damage on the human body.

As soon as the situation in northern Morocco was stabilized, Major Hopkins paid Emile a visit in the ship. He was pleased to see Emile sitting up in bed using his right hand to feed himself. He recognized Saul and was pleased to see a familiar face.

"It's nice to see you, Saul. I'm sorry that I left you in such a bad situation," Emile said, pushing his tray to one side. "Tell me, Saul, how bad was it at the hilltop?"

"Colonel Ranta," Saul replied, "you look great. The men have been worried about you. I talked to the head surgeon. He informed me that you're doing well under the circumstances. We lost thirty men killed and forty wounded in that last fight when you were wounded. We held the hill, and I'm so proud of the men. You trained them well, Colonel. Your old job is available as soon as they finish with you here on the ship. I'll be glad to take back my old position."

Emile smiled. He liked this young studious officer and was glad to have him at his side during the difficult baptism of fire on the sand plains of Morocco and Algiers. "I hope that my leg improves so that I can return to duty... The doctors are still noncommittal about my left leg."

Saul placed a comforting hand on his shoulder and said, "You're in my prayers, Colonel, and I speak for every man in the battalion. We were all proud to serve under your leadership. I was anxious to see how you were doing and to convey to you the fact that every man in the battalion signed the petition for you to be awarded the Medal of Honor. Your actions above and beyond warrant that medal, Sir."

Touched by Saul's statement, Emile turned his head. Tears stained the white pillow. "I blame myself for the loss of so many good men," he answered in a low voice. "I could have fallen back with the rest of the regiment, but..."

"Colonel, you did what few would have had the courage to do. You saw the value of the hilltop and challenged the large German contingent that was holding it. In the long run, it has already saved countless Allied lives by eliminating a vital strong point that was responsible for the death of hundreds of good men. The fact that the men followed you without hesitation is a tribute to your leadership. If you had retreated with the rest of the regiment, our battalion would probably have been decimated by artillery directed from that hilltop. I did not want to intrude on your rest, Sir. I speak for the battalion when I wish you a rapid recovery. It was a pleasure to serve with you. Goodbye, Sir."

"Thanks for coming, Saul. I apologize for being so emotional," Emile replied.

"No apology is necessary, Sir."

Shortly after Major Hopkins' visit, Emile was transferred to an Air Corps DC-3 that had been converted to accommodate wounded soldiers. He was flown across the Atlantic to Walter Reed Hospital in Washington, D.C. The first day of his arrival, Emile was notified that the Medal of Honor recommended by Major Hopkins and signed by every member of his battalion, had been approved. He had flown half-way around the world in a medicated state of awareness.

It was like a bad dream to him until one morning he awoke to see his daughter, Faye, bending over him. She kissed him on the forehead. He felt the kiss and instantly recognized her. Tears formed in the corner of his eyes. She wiped them with a soft tissue.

"You've had us all worried, Dad," she said in a quiet voice.

"It's so nice to see you, Faye. They've had me medicated a lot between North Africa and the hospital here," he held out his right hand to her. "It's been a long time…"

"Mom called to tell me that you had been transferred to Walter Reed. I was able to get connections on the train. They were packed with service men and women coming and going. We only get a few gallons of gasoline per week, so I drive the car sparingly. I walk to school. Mom told me to tell you that she was going to see you sometime this week," Faye told him.

"You look a little drawn, Faye. Is everything going okay for you at school?" Emile asked his daughter. She had dark circles under her eyes. He was concerned for her.

She avoided his penetrating stare. "Well, school has been demanding. We're short of help, and the enrollment has increased ten percent since I started," she explained. "Don't worry, I'm adapting to the routine. I really like teaching the fourth grade. The kids are great. Most of the families have someone in the armed services and, even at their young age, they worry for their loved ones. This war is going to be a long, ugly affair… but then, my Father knows that better than anyone. I'm so proud of your Medal of Honor. It's given to very few soldiers for heroic acts. Alpha and I are not surprised that our father has earned our country's highest honor." She squeezed his hand.

"If you don't stop, I'll get a swelled head, Honey. I'm honored to receive the award, but in all honesty, there are many who deserve it more but remain unrecognized. Every Ranger in my battalion earned the same award, so I will receive it for them. They started out as young inexperienced men and very shortly became stalwart defenders of our liberties and safety. They've earned my respect and affection. I hope the people are worthy of their sacrifice."

Faye visited with her father until he appeared tired. She left for the hospitality room made available to her at Fort Meyers, across the Potomac in Arlington. It's home base for the very special guards at the Tomb of the Unknown Soldier. The next day she visited her father and told him that her mother was coming the first of next week.

"I have to leave tonight," she explained. "My classes start tomorrow morning at eight o'clock. I'll try to make it next week, Dad." She found her father a little more alert. She had put on a little more lipstick and rouge to give her better color. He noticed the difference.

"You look a little more rested today, Honey. You've got to promise your Dad that you'll take better care of yourself. It's enough that I'm in the hospital. You and your mother should not worry about me. The doctors tell me that my wounds will heal. I'll be back with my command within a month. I'm impatient to get out of this bed," Emile confessed.

She smiled at him and saw some of that old gleam in his eyes that meant that he was determined about something. "I'll write Alpha to tell him how you're doing, Dad."

They reminisced for a few hours before Faye left to catch her train for New Hampshire. Emile was uncomfortable about something Faye was keeping from him. He could not get her to tell him what was wrong. She used the workload at the school as an excuse, but he did not buy it. Ever since she was a little girl she was capable of working long hours regardless of how hard the job was. He made up his mind that he'd find out what was wrong when Bonnie came for a visit.

That next morning, Bonnie entered his hospital room with a flushed look on her face and cringed when she saw how seriously he was wounded. He was resting with his eyes closed. She bent over him and whispered in his ear, "Hello, Em."

He recognized that voice and looked into her blue eyes. "Bonnie, what a nice surprise."

"I got in Washington early this morning and had a chance to talk with Faye before she left for New Hampshire. She seemed upset about something. Did you two have words, Em?"

"No, Bonnie, she refused to tell me what's bothering her," Emile answered. "I thought you might know something."

"No, she hasn't confided anything to me for quite a while. I get the impression that she's trying to avoid me, and I'm worried about her," Bonnie explained. She studied the lines on his face and was shocked at the deep-sunken eyes that looked at her. "I was sorry to hear about your injuries, Em. Your body has absorbed more than any person I know. I pray that this will be the last time you'll have to go back into combat." She placed her hand on his forehead. "You still have a slight fever. What do the doctors tell you about your wounds?"

"They did tell me that I'd be able to return to duty with my battalion within a month or so. I feel better than I look, Bonnie. I was sorry to hear about Lewis. Our losses before this is over will be horrendous. We were so unprepared for war, but we're learning a lot as we progress. A lot of mistakes were made fighting two powerful enemies on two different continents."

Bonnie sighed and said, "Lewis and I didn't have as good a marriage as we had."

"Bonnie, I really don't want to get into the past. We've all made mistakes in our lives. If I had to do it over again, I'd probably do the same thing. It's important for you to know that I love the Army and I've never regretted my career. It probably was selfish of me. The kids and you were hurt the most by my long absences…but that's in the past and we can't do anything about it now."

"I didn't mean to dredge up old memories. God knows I've got my share of regrets. I've been getting wonderful letters from Alpha. He's a lot like you, Em. I'm so proud of him. The day he left for boot camp was a bad one for me. I offered to stay with Faye for a while, but she made all kind of excuses, so I withdrew my offer. She worries me too, Em."

"Will you promise to keep me informed about Faye and Alpha?"

"Yes, I promise... both of the children have told me that you've found someone special in your life. You deserve more peace and love than I gave you..."

He was surprised to hear that statement from her. "I appreciate that, Bonnie. She's an Army nurse and I enjoy her company." He did not elaborate about the relationship and found it strange that she was still concerned for him. Over the years they had been married, she had been more concerned about herself. She was not really selfish, for she willingly went without in order to provide for the children. He often thought it stemmed from the very modest surroundings she grew up in. Her father had been an alcoholic while her mother worked tirelessly for the welfare of the children, and to keep the family together. As a young child, Bonnie often went without a lot of things other friends took for granted.

He enjoyed Bonnie's visit. They had talked and reminisced about the good times, and there were many in their lives. When it came time for her to catch her train to Vermont, she bent over Emile and kissed him on the forehead. "I'll keep you informed about the children. Good-bye, Em. You'll always be in my prayers."

Emile thanked her for the visit and watched her walk out of the ward. She paused at the door and turned to wave to him. He could see that she was crying...

Chapter Seventeen

Faye came to the hospital dressed in a dark blue trench coat. It was a cold, blustery day that threatened to snow. She accompanied her father. Several meticulously dressed soldiers escorted them from the hospital to a 1941 Ford Army sedan. They efficiently assisted him from the wheelchair into the sedan and out of the vehicle once they arrived at the White House. The ceremony in the Oval Office was somber and brief. Emile was the last man to receive the Medal of Honor from President Roosevelt. He rolled his wheelchair in front of Emile and carefully placed the sash of the Medal over his head, and briefly read Emile's citation which cover events that took place as the Rangers were scaling the cliffs in Normandy.

The President then made eye contact with the men and continued: "My fellow Americans, I can honestly tell you that the presentation of the Medal of Honor to such courageous men is a privilege and an honor that I truly cherish. I thank you for the people of this great nation. Your valor on the field of battle in the defense of our country is an inspiration to all of us. Thank you for your service, and May God Bless all of you."

Everyone present at the ceremony were struck by the tired and drawn look on the President's face. The men were escorted out of the Oval Office. Faye had witnessed the ceremony with moist eyes. How proud she was of her father. He was the oldest soldier to receive the medal, and she prayed that he would not have to face the guns again.

Emile was quiet and reflective as he was transported back to the hospital. He was tired and wanted to rest. The nurses helped him change into a hospital gown and get into the bed, leaving his Medal about his neck.

"You look tired, Dad," Faye told him. "While you rest, I'm going to get a cup of coffee from the cafeteria. I didn't have a chance to eat breakfast before I caught the train. I'll see you a little later."

"Okay, Honey. I am a little tired. Later this afternoon, you and I will have to talk."

She knew what he wanted to talk about. "You rest easy, Dad. I'll see you after you wake up..."

Faye knew that this visit was going to be difficult. She was dreading the confrontation. She thought that she could discuss her situation better with her mother, but, so far, she had not been able to. The past few months had been the most agonizing of her life, and she was reluctant to burden her father with her problem. Now, it could not be avoided. The cafeteria was crowded. She selected a bowl of chicken soup and shared a seat with a wounded soldier who was having trouble cutting his steak with one arm missing. He was embarrassed as she sat down. Faye saw that he was troubled and offered to help him. "May I help you, Sergeant?"

The soldier smiled and pushed the plate in front of her. "Thank you, Ma'am. I didn't think about cutting the meat when I selected it at the counter. Eventually I'll be fitted with a new arm and be able to do a lot for things for myself."

She noted that he was self-conscious of his condition. "I understand, Sergeant. My father is here in the hospital. He was wounded in Africa. It's my pleasure to help where I can. This steak looks good." She cut it into small pieces and pushed the plate to the soldier.

"Thank you, Ma'am. It smells good doesn't it?" the soldier replied.

"Yes, it does, Sergeant," Faye replied, sipping her coffee.

"One of the nurses told me that a soldier from our floor of the hospital had just been awarded the Medal of Honor. That's the most respected award in the military. Only a select few receive it," the Sergeant told her.

She was thinking about her father. Over the years they had been close. He was easy to talk to, and she often had confided things in her life with him that she would have been

123

uncomfortable to do with her, mother. She slowly drank her coffee and wished the Sergeant good luck. She silently asked God to help her as she returned to her father's room.

Emile had taken a short nap while she was gone and was ready to eat the lunch that an orderly had placed on his side table. He had just finished the cup of custard when Faye walked into his room. She was mentally prepared for the confrontation that was about to take place.

"I see that you ate most of your lunch, Dad," she said, rolling the stand way from his bedside.

"The food really isn't bad, Faye." He carefully watched her take a seat close to bed so that they could see each other. "I'm sure that it's warm enough in here that you don't need to keep that trench coat on, Faye."

"Ah" she announced to herself. He was prepared to discuss her situation! She felt like running out of the room, but stood up to remove the coat, placing it at the foot of his bed. She placed a chair close to his bedside and sat down. Her pregnancy was obvious to her father.

"How far along are you, Faye?" he asked in a wavering voice, uncertain if he should be disappointed or pleased with her condition. Her obvious efforts to conceal it from him bothered him the most.

"About seven months," she answered in a firm voice, avoiding his penetrating eyes.

"Can you tell me who the father is?"

"I can't do that, Father."

"Is it someone I know?" he asked, aware of her extreme discomfort in discussing her situation.

"I can't tell you that either, Father."

"Do you mean that you don't know the man or that you won't tell me who he is?"

"Father," she cried, filled with anguish and pain. "I know that it may sound strange to you. At some time in the future, I'll be able to inform you. Right now, I just can't do that, so please don't ask me again."

"Does your mother know?"

"I've avoided her because I knew that she would be asking the same questions that you are. Right now my life is in turmoil.

Hopefully I'll have the baby during the Christmas and New Year breaks from school. That way I won't have to lose a lot of time from my teaching obligations."

Emile was concerned about the agonizing ordeal that his daughter was experiencing. Yet, she seemed determined to go through the scrutiny alone and that angered him. He was angered as well as concerned for her welfare and felt powerless to help her in any way possible. He cautiously asked, "Are you going to have your mother stay with you when your time is close? You'll need someone to help you, or is the father of the child prepared to step up to the responsibility and do what any father would normally do?"

Faye responded quickly to his request. "No, the father is not aware of my condition, and I will not tell him, so stop asking that question," she bluntly told him.

"I find that unacceptable, Faye. What are you going to do?"

She made eye-to-eye contact with him and slowly and distinctly said, "I've made up my mind to place the child for adoption just as soon as it's born…"

"My God, Faye. You've got to be more responsible than that for the child…" Emile replied, raising his voice.

"Father," Faye interrupted her father, standing beside the bed. "I've given this more thought than either you or Mother can imagine. It's the only out for me."

The room was filled with tension. Both Emile and Faye were overwhelmed with emotions. His first thoughts were for his daughter, Faye, who was the offspring of another man. That fact had given him one of the most hurtful and most difficult moments in his life. He thought that he had successfully put that aside forever, for he loved this young lady he called his daughter. Now the same ugly thoughts flowed through his mind. He could not ignore the pain they inflicted. "I can't help but recall how I felt when your mother first told me that she was pregnant with you. Those same images really hurt, but… Like mother, like daughter…" He angrily cried, "You can't put the baby up for adoption, Faye… You'll regret it, believe me."

He regretted the words as soon as they were spoken, and they generated an angry response from Faye such as he had never experienced from any other human being. "At last, after all these years of pretending to love me, the truth comes out. There was always a small part of me that questioned if you were sincere. Slowly over the years, those dark thoughts were successfully pushed out of my mind because I believed that you truly loved and respected me... Now..."

"Faye, Faye...please don't say anymore, forgive me. I did not mean to hurt you...Oh God believe me...my love for you was sincere, and I've always been proud, watching you grow into a fine young lady. Please, don't ever doubt it."

She was oblivious to his pleas for reason. "In times of crisis the truth usually comes to the surface just as it has now with you," Faye stopped to take a deep breath and continued with her voice filled with rancor and pain. ""I've made up my mind. I'm having the child adopted. I considered an abortion, but this child has a right to life. I'll give it that, but I don't want anything to do with him or her...and that's final!"

Emile was speechless. A nurse entered the room to see the cause of the angry voices she heard at the nurse's station.

"I apologize, nurse," Faye exclaimed, grasping her coat from the bed. "I'm leaving now."

"No...Don't go like this, Faye...Please."

"There's nothing more to say, Father. As usual, you've had the last word... Goodbye. I do wish you well, but I won't be back." With that, she quickly left the ward.

"Faye...Faye..." Emile helplessly cried, extending a hand to her as she left. "Please..."

The nurse gave him a sedative to calm him down. The last thing he remembered was the vision of Faye at the door, turning to him and waving. Then she was gone.

Emile was kept under sedation for the next twenty-four hours. When he awoke, he was surprised to see Bonnie sitting beside his bed. She had a frustrated look on her face.

"Have you spoken to Faye?" he asked with a strained voice.

"Yes, Em. I spoke to her shortly after she left the hospital. I didn't know she was pregnant until she told me over the phone. She also told me that she was not going to abort the child, but was going to put it up for adoption immediately after birth. She's already signed papers for that to take place." Bonnie was more disturbed about the break between Emile and Faye than she was about Faye's condition.

He processed what she told him and replied, "We can't let her go through this thing on her own, Bonnie. My God, what can we do? She told me the same things, and left outraged at me because I made the unkind remark that she was like her mother in many ways."

"Emile, you dragged that incident out of the past and hung it around her neck. How could you after all the good years the two of you have had together?"

"I know…I know. I lashed out at her when I should have taken her in my arms to tell her that I only want what is good for her. "Emile was still haunted by the magnitude of the rupture he had created with his vicious tongue. She had been the joy of his life. He turned away from Bonnie so that she could not see the tears bursting for release. He never felt so helpless in his life.

Bonnie was concerned at how deeply he was troubled. "Right now, Em, you've got to get well again. I'll take a train to Vermont and try to make contact with Faye. I'd go to stay with her if she would let me. She needs someone even if she denies it. I can't stand by and watch her handle such a delicate situation all by herself. I'll keep in touch with you, Em. How long do the doctors think it will take you to return to duty?"

In the midst of the chaos around him he was relieved that Bonnie was willing to do what most mothers would do. "I think you should insist on being with her. Please convey my apologies for the cruel words I unleashed on her without cause. Tell her I do love her… God I wish I could retract those words."

"The Faye that we both love is consumed with despair right now, but I would not be surprised that deep in her heart she knows that you did not mean to hurt her as deeply as you did. I'll keep in touch with you, Em. I've got a train to catch. I'll try to see you again before you leave the hospital. It's so hard to travel now. The trains and buses are packed with people, mostly in uniform. Good-bye, Em." She bent over to kiss him. "Try not to worry, just get well."

"Thanks, Bonnie. I'll be looking forward to word from you. Do tell Faye that I love her more than she knows."

"I will. Until next time, Em."

"Until next time, Bonnie." He watched her leave the room and wiped the tears from his cheeks.

Chapter Eighteen

January 1, 1943

Emile left the Walter Reed Hospital for non-hazardous duty in England. Experienced military officers were scarce. Normally he would have been retired from the service, but he responded well to physical therapy. He was assigned to the large United States Army contingent in England developing plans for the invasion of Fortress Europe to conquer Germany. It was a dauntless task that would eventually order the most powerful military force the world has ever known into Europe to destroy Germany and to free those countries they had so ruthlessly overpowered and occupied. He was capable of carrying out normal executive duties for a few months. After that, he would resume command of one of the Ranger battalions. He was proud to be back with the hardy Rangers and participated in continuous training exercises when they were not accompanying British Commando raids against German strongholds along the French coast. Those hit-and-run tactics would force the Germans to maintain large numbers of troops at those strong points, precluding their being used in an amphibious invasion of the British Isles.

Before he left for England Bonnie had visited him several times while he was recuperating at the hospital. She was able to keep him abreast of how Faye was getting along. Emile wrote several letters addressed to Faye at the house. They came back unopened with the same stamp – Return to Sender. His calls were not answered either. She obviously hated him, and it hurt…it hurt bad!

He was sick with worry and was uncomfortable leaving the states for England, knowing that the situation with Faye

129

was unresolved. She had completely severed relations with her father. Bonnie told him that she had immediately placed her healthy baby girl for adoption. She did not even hold the child in her arms. A nurse had shown her the baby and asked for a final confirmation about the adoption. Bonnie had been with her at that moment. Faye heard the baby cry as the nurse walked out the door, and buried her face in the pillow, crying for a long time.

Emile left for overseas duty mentally and physically challenged. Bonnie had tried to assure him that she would try her best to heal the breech that had come between him and Faye. He had little hope that it would change. He entered his duties with a passion and a vigor that helped to temporarily blank all the bad thoughts from his mind. The nights were still long and filled with regret.

The proposed invasion of Sicily was called Operation Husky. It came shortly after the large German Army in Africa had surrendered. Emile's Ranger battalion was assigned to lead the invasion July 10, 1943. Once a safe beachhead had been secured, the Rangers were ordered to penetrate inland as far as possible to secure and/or destroy bridges leading to the coast. It was a bloody and vicious fight. The Germans and Italians stubbornly resisted. Emile lost ten percent of his Rangers killed or wounded in the first week of the operation. Sicily proved to be a more difficult fight for the Allies than Africa.

Italy was invaded early in September, 1943. Now the costliest engagements of the war took place. Italy was ready to surrender, but the large number of German troops still in the country were reinforced. Prime Minister Churchill called the invasion of Italy the "soft underbelly" of mainland Europe, thinking that it might be a good way to obtain a foothold on the continent. Germany was determined to make that operation as difficult as possible. For months, Allied troops blasted their way up the boot of Italy. Again, Rangers frequently were used as point troops to lead the way. They were also assigned several behind-the-lines operations to knock out strongholds that resisted artillery and heavy caliber Navy batteries.

Heavy casualties for his Rangers gave Emile cause to intensely review every order he gave to the men so as to be certain that casualties were as light as possible. Orders were orders, and he found no way to accomplish the missions without casualties. Those losses were weighing heavily on his mind. The battalion was slowly reaching the point where they needed to be relieved. Sixty percent casualties and extreme fatigue minimized their ability to seize objectives as efficiently as they had done in the past. Emile requested that they be recalled for a rest period.

He returned to England with the battalion which was badly in need of replacements of man and material. Rest and a diet free of field rations was required. They had fought courageously under Emile's leadership. He was proud of their exceptional performance. Once the Rangers and the British Commandoes were recognized as elite troops, the General Staff acknowledged that they should be used sparingly for those difficult assignments that required highly trained and motivated troops. Using them as traditional front-line troops was a waste of manpower.

Once Emile got his troopers established in suitable quarters, he received an order to report to the newly formed Allied Expeditionary Force for the invasion of mainland Europe at their headquarters in London. He was amazed at the destruction in the city from German bombers. He showed his ID at the main gate to the headquarters and was directed to the office of General Omar Bradley, commander of the First Army Corps. Emile's Rangers had been attached to his command, and like most who served under the General, admired him. Emile was warmly received by a young aide who showed him to the General's office.

"The General and the staff have been pleased with the performance of your Ranger battalion, Sir." The Lieutenant opened a door and directed Emile to enter the office.

General Bradley was expecting him, and came around his desk to greet him. "Colonel Ranta, I'm glad to see you. You and your men have performed well under extreme conditions. I'm sure that you and your men deserve a rest from combat. Please sit down, Colonel," he said, pointing to a chair beside his large desk.

Emile removed his hat and sat down. "The men made it easy, General. I was proud to command them," he replied.

"Colonel Ranta, I do not know how to announce to you, but I have the unpleasant duty to inform you that your son, Corporal Alpha Ranta, has been killed in action in Italy." The news hit Emile like a sledgehammer. He was now experiencing the trauma that thousands of parents have had to endure when notifications of death in the line of duty are sent to homes across the country. He had a feeling that this visit could involve Alpha, and he prayed that it was for injuries instead of death. He was wrong; his son was dead! He was unprepared for the emptiness that consumed him, and he could never anticipate the anguish the news created. Completely overwhelmed by the finality of his son's death, Emile held his head in his two hands and wept.

General Bradley rose from his desk and laid two comforting hands on Emile's shoulders. "This profession we've chosen, Colonel, asks much from those who serve. I never knew how to inform a parent of the death of a loved one without imparting massive grief and pain. It's one of the most difficult duties of being a soldier. "

Emile could picture the last time he saw Alpha before he left for basic training. He was anxious and ready to do his part. His decision to volunteer made Emile proud of him. Now all that he had was memories, he yearned to embrace his son one more time.

"Your wife will be notified within days, Colonel," the General told him. "If I had the power, I'd erase the grief you're experiencing. These notification duties are a difficult task for most soldiers, but, alas, it is minor compared to the devastation the words 'killed in action' convey to a parent or loved one. Forgive me for being the bearer of such bad news, Colonel. "

Emile knew that this kind, soft-spoken man was one of the most respected officers in the Army. "I didn't think it would hurt so much, General."

"How could it be any other way, Colonel? I wish that I could give you orders to return home for a few days, but we're in the midst of a monumental task here in England that requires maximum effort from all of us," General Bradley told him.

"I understand, Sir. Training my Rangers for the invasion of Europe is a job I've been preparing for all these years in the Army. In a way it will help take my mind off my son's loss," Emile replied, standing to leave. "I do have a request to make, General."

"If it's within my power, I'll grant your request, Colonel."

Emile turned to confront the General. "My ex-wife is in Vermont, and the Division has her address. Would you also have them send a letter of notification to my daughter at my home address in Berlin, New Hampshire? We've had a family disagreement and it would mean a lot to me if you could send her word of Alpha's death, and remind her that her father loves her very much and is going to be very busy until the war is over."

"Consider it done, Colonel Ranta."

Emile returned to his quarters on the coast of England filled with heartache. His world was disassembling. He picked up his mail and told his executive officer that he did not want to be disturbed for the rest of the evening. He went through the mail separating the normal intra-service mail from his personal letters. He had only one, and that was from Cora. He removed his jacket and sat on the army cot to read the letter:

Somewhere in the Pacific Ocean

December 28, 1943

Dear Emile,

I apologize for not writing more often. I've been assigned to a large Army Hospital Ship in the Pacific. That's all I can tell you now, and I'm sure you understand.

It's been a long time since I heard from you. You're always in my prayers. This ugly war is turning out to be a very costly conflict. Young men in their prime of life are being lost to us at an alarming rate and we've barely started. I'm not sure how long I can emotionally handle the carnage that is taking place. The wounded men in the wards are fabulous. Many are showing more courage in the wards than on the battlefield. That brotherhood of warriors holds them together. No one suffers alone. They circle around those more seriously wounded. Their compassion for each other is a sight to witness. I'm so proud to serve them.

Tonight, I experienced one of the most beautiful sunsets I've ever seen. It covered the whole horizon with a red haze that held everybody in awe of its beauty. I thought of you and would have liked to have shared it with you, Emile.

Until next time. Whenever that is in this world of uncertainty, I send my love to you across the miles.

Cora

Emile read the letter a second time and wrote a short reply informing her of Alpha's death. He was unable to tell her what he was doing or even where he was. He found some comfort when he shared the fact that Alpha was with him when he first met Cora beside the Kennebec River in Maine with a flat tire. That seemed a long time ago and it brought tears to his eyes. He had so enjoyed his son. They were not just father and son, they were also buddies. Cora and Emile had not had time to establish a deeper relationship with each other, but what time they did share together had been enough for Emile to believe that he had fallen in love with her. He felt a strong need for someone to be a part of his dreams for tomorrow so that he could erase all of the debilitating effect brutal combat was having on him. He finished the letter and stared at the dark waters of the English Channel. It sent shivers up and down his spine. He knew that someday soon he and his elite battalion were going to cross it. The ominous defenses the Germans had created on the distant shores were frightening. He prayed for the ability and strength needed to lead his troops against the full resources of the enemy on that distant shore. It was the Germans who were responsible for the death of his son. Emile prayed that he could make the enemy pay retribution for taking his beloved son away from him. He was anxious to yield the "hand of steel" Churchill had promised the German army for all of the death and destruction emanating from the evil nation. A powerful rage grew in Emile's soul; he would avenge his son's death.

Chapter Nineteen

Spring of 1944

The first thing that Emile did after his nerve shattering visit to General Bradley's office was to make sure that his men were taken care of. They had earned a short rest from the trauma of combat. He was assured that the men could take short liberties in London. The USO clubs were favorite locations where they could get a decent meal and a good cup of coffee for both enlisted men and officers. No alcohol was allowed, and fraternization with the ladies who worked at the clubs was discouraged.

The American troops were a long way from home, and the English people took the brash American soldiers into their homes and hearts. The air was filled with uncertainty. In that period of unsure destinations and tomorrows, Vera Lynn, a British singer, with the voice of an angel, left her romantic mark on the Americans' memories with her bittersweet ballads of home, heartbreak, and separation. Her rendition of the beautiful ballad: *We'll Meet Again* so touched their hearts that, years later, they could still remember the poignant words... "We'll meet again, don't know where, don't know when..." They evoked warm memories of home, miles across the dark Atlantic Ocean.

Emile was kept busy with daily conferences where plans were developed for the invasion of occupied France as a stepping stone to the destruction of Germany. It would be the largest amphibious invasion in history. The powerful military effort would have to be aimed at the northern coast of France, a short distance across the English Channel, where the Germans had constructed massive coastal batteries capable of blowing any invasion force out of the waters. Those veterans of combat with the Germans knew that the initial assault on the continent would be extremely costly in men and machinery. The major battle of the World War would be won or lost within the first twenty-four hours. Large numbers of German troops and armored forces were stationed within striking distance of the coast.

Once the major planners of the Allied invasion forces determined where they would launch the attack, they envisioned that thousands of men and ships would be committed. The Allied invasion was given the code name *Overlord*. They all agreed upon a plan to land forces on the coast of Normandy directly across the Channel from the Isle of Wight. The code names for the beaches to be assaulted were *Utah, Omaha, Gold, Juno,* and *Sword,* all east of the Cotentin Peninsula. Pointe du Hoc was a prominent cliff one hundred feet high overlooking the landing beaches. It was the highest point between *Omaha* and *Utah.* The Germans had constructed heavy casements for six 155mm cannons capable of destroying the allied landings and the ships ten miles out to sea. They had to be eliminated before the main landings took place.

The destruction of these artillery batteries became a high priority. The mission to destroy the batteries was given to the 2nd and 5th Ranger battalions. Emile was ordered to work up a plan of action for the elimination of the guns. It was a task many called impossible. They had tried bombing the area, but the guns survived the aerial assaults. By the time large Naval cannons could be brought to bear on the cliff, the guns were capable of destroying the battleships and cruisers. The planners anticipated paratroopers, but dismissed the plans as too risky. That left an assault from the beach. The Rangers would have to fight their way up the cliffs. Emile and his small staff thought it was a suicide mission! Even with the best of possibilities, it was going to be a costly attack for the Rangers. One officer remarked that three women armed with brooms could keep the Rangers from reaching the top. There were no easy solutions to the problem, and there were no other American troops trained for such a mission.

The main planners assured Emile that he would have the highest priority for firepower. Whatever he needed to accomplish the mission, he would be granted. The relief of his Rangers would immediately take place as soon as land troops were beginning to move inland from *Omaha* and *Utah*.

Once the decision was made, and sufficient orders given to the Ranger components, Emile began a rigid training program for the battalions. He assembled an officer conference and described in detail what was expected of them. The company commanders were responsible for executing the training program. Emile told them that he and his executive officer were going to work with the Navy support force they were attached to. They planned to come up with a specific timetable of events and they wanted to be absolutely certain that their Naval components were working with the same plans and timetable.

The day after they received their initial orders, Emile and Major Tom Huntley, a recent Officer Candidate School graduate, went to the Naval Yard near the Isle of Wight to confer with the Navy destroyer captain that had been assigned to their Point du Hoc operation. Captain Winslow of the destroyer, USS *Satterlee* warmly received them in the officers wardroom.

"I expected a visit from the Army after receiving orders that we are to provide support while you Rangers scale the cliff to secure the gun emplacements at topside. My God, what a task you and your men have!"

Emile smiled. "This is our battalion executive officer, Major Huntley. I'm Colonel Ranta. Yes, we drew a difficult mission, but if we're lucky, and have adequate support from the Navy, we should be able to do the job. Major Huntley and I wanted to make sure that we are all working from the same program. Our lives are in your hands while we climb the cliffs. How close will you get to the beach area with the destroyer, Captain Winslow?"

"I've been notified that a British destroyer will also accompany our ship and the landing crafts, transporting your Army troops to the beach. We will not be able to get as close as you would like, Colonel. I do not want to beach the ship. That will make us a sitting duck for the German gunners ashore. The landing craft will of course take you to the beach. I understand that several amphibious DUKWS have also been assigned to your troops. They are capable of traveling across the beachhead directly to the cliffs."

"I know that, Captain," Emile replied. "We'll be using the landing craft and the DUKWS as platforms for the rocket launchers to fire grapples and ropes up the cliffs. Once we start the climb, my Rangers will be helpless and will depend on your fire power to suppress any effort by the enemy to fire down on us or to lob grenades over the edge of the cliffs. We also need to be using the same radio frequencies for immediate and clear communications. That is crucial for our survival."

Emile knew that he was asking a lot from the Captain, but the lives of his Rangers were in their hands, and he wanted no misunderstandings between the two services.

"I understand your situation, Colonel. I would be doing the same thing in your place. Let me assure you that we are proud that we can assist your courageous Rangers during this monumental assault on the Continent of Europe. I have a suggestion that may help your situation. There is a Coast Guard Cutter tied up at the pier to our left. It's a smaller ship with a more shallow draft than our destroyer. I'm not sure if they have been given specific orders for the invasion. You can check with them. I've found them to be the most 'can-do' ship in England. Those Coasties are fabulous sailors, and they run a tight ship."

"That sounds like a good idea, Captain. I saw it on our way to your destroyer. We'll pay them a visit. Thanks for assuring me that we can work together in a spirit of cooperation. We'll check in with the Coast Guard. Thanks for the tip." Emile saluted the Captain and left the destroyer.

The Coast Guard cutter was a smaller ship, but it had sleek lines and appeared to be heavily armed. Emile and Tom Huntley walked up the gangplank and asked the young Coast Guard officer on the deck for permission to come aboard.

"Permission granted, Colonel," He saluted and continued: "Our Captain is not on the ship, Sir. How may I help you?"

Emile and Tom stepped on the deck and saluted the officer of the day. "I'm Colonel Ranta and this is Major Huntley. We wanted to discuss with whoever is in command about the possibility of utilizing your cutter for support of a mission assigned to our Ranger battalion."

"I've just recently been assigned to the cutter and am not privy to our task. The Captain left with the exec officer for an appointment at the Allied Command Headquarters in London. I see that our chief gunner is up on the bridge. Probably you should speak to him."

Emile saw a middle-aged chief petty officer on the bridge and approached him. The chief came to attention and saluted Emile and Tom. They returned the salute. Emile was uncertain if the chief could help them or not. "Chief, I'm Colonel Ranta and this is my exec officer, Major Huntley. We are interested to learn if your Coast Guard cutter would be available to assist us in a mission we've been ordered to carry out."

"Well, I'm only chief gunnery officer, but the Captain keeps us well informed as to what is expected of us. He is probably in the process of receiving orders as we speak. Maybe I can assist you if you have any questions."

Emile explained what their orders were and told him that the shallow draft of the ship made it a valuable choice to lend fire support for their mission. "We're concerned that the destroyers will not get as close to the beachhead as we would like."

The chief understood what Emile told him. "Follow me to the forward gun turret, Sirs. We were offered two quad-fifty-caliber machine guns for installation on our forward deck. That's one of the things the Captain is discussing with the Naval staff as we speak. We do have room between the main three-inch cannon turret to mount such weapons to the deck. They would certainly be useful to support an operation such as you've been assigned."

"I'm familiar with that type of mount, Chief. It's a potent support weapon," Emile exclaimed, excited about the potential. "How close to the shore could this ship get?"

"We've given support to several amphibious landings where the Captain actually beached the ship. In Italy we got to within twenty feet of the dry beachhead." The Chief was looking at the forward turret mount. "If we were given the assignment to support you, we might be able to modify this mount so that we could elevate the cannon to act more like a mortar. A shim of a few inches would make a lot of difference with its trajectory."

"Chief, that's a great idea, that would give us excellent fire support while we make the climb up the ropes. You've been a lot of help. Please tell your Captain what we were looking for and tell him to contact me at any time, day or night." Emile gave him a card with their address and radio call numbers. "I'll be looking forward to visit with your Captain. Thanks for your time, Chief. Your Coast Guard cutter is a beautiful vessel. I hope we can add you to the team."

"I'll tell the Captain, Colonel. We came here to serve and to do our part. You Rangers have a great reputation for carrying out difficult jobs. I wish you luck."

Emile and Tom left the cutter relieved, hoping that they could lay claim to the Coast Guard ship for their mission. Both officers liked their "can-do" attitude.

"I think I'll check with the bomber crews that have been designated as our air-support team," Emile told Tom. "You return to our bivouac. Make sure that the men continue their rope climbing exercises, and check on the London Fire Department. Our orders specify that they are equipping one of our landing crafts with an aerial ladder capable of reaching one hundred feet."

Tom saluted Emile. "I wish you luck with the Air Force. It would be great if we could fly over the objective of our mission. There's nothing like having a good view of what we're up against."

"If I can arrange that, I'll call for you to join me, Tom." Emile replied.

The next day Emile and Tom were called to participate in a bomb run against the Point. They met with the young pilot of the Douglas A-20 bomber-night fighter aircraft that was going to raid the Point. A bird's eye view of their target was anxiously anticipated by the two Rangers. The pilot told them that the Havoc aircraft was one of the most successful aircraft in the Army Air Corps. It was fast and very maneuverable much like a single-engine fighter plane. It was capable of carrying a bomb load, and with its four nose-mounted 20 mm cannons, it packed a deadly punch. The pilot told them that the plane was a joy to fly and responded quickly to control. It had a three-man crew.

It was a clear day with good visibility. Emile and Tom were welcomed into the small cockpit area where they had excellent visibility. They took off at a field west of London and within a few minutes they were over the English Channel. The pilot flew directly across from the Isle of Wight to the Point on the horizon. Emile was straining to see the cliffs that quickly rose in front of them.

The pilot pointed to the cliffs. "That's our target. We're going to make a straight-in run on the top of the cliff to drop our bomb load on the gun emplacements. Then we'll reverse course to make a low-level strafing run with our four cannons in the nose of the aircraft. That should give you a decent picture of what's on top of the cliffs."

It was noisy in the cockpit and Emile nodded his head to acknowledge what the pilot had said. He was mesmerized by the steepness and height of the cliffs. It was going to be a tough climb!

The bomb run was completed, and the pilot quickly made a u-turn and started the strafing run at fifty feet above the ground. The heavy cannons stitched four rows across the top of the cliff area, kicking up a cloud of dust and material. The bombs did not seem to make any difference to the encasements. The cannons were unscathed!!

The pilot then made several passes close to the cliffs while the single tail gunner sprayed the topside with machine-gun fire. Emile and Tom memorized the layout at the top of the cliff and were worried about the height and steepness of the climb they would have to make under enemy fire!

Emile and Tom thanked the pilot and crew of the aircraft as they climbed into their Jeep. Their view of the Point was a sobering experience, and they were silent all the way back to their quarters.

Chapter Twenty

Emile instantly ordered the men to concentrate on rope-climbing. Their ability to successfully scale the cliffs hinged on that skill. In his heart he knew that he was going to lose a lot of good men and he was sickened by the thought. The battalion trained on the cliffs at the Isle of Wight. On a clear day they could see Point du Hoc. It served as an incentive to train harder. The cliffs became a grim factor in the men's dreams. The invasion date was set for June 5th. Emile had completed all of the paperwork for the three companies he was commanding the day of the invasion when a courier pulled his motorcycle up to the tent entrance and asked for a Colonel Ranta. A soldier nearby pointed to Emile's tent. "The Colonel should be inside the tent."

The courier took a large envelope from his dispatch case and announced himself: "Mail for Colonel Ranta."

"Come inside, soldier. I'm Colonel Ranta.

"This packet just came into our center, Sir," the courier replied, saluting and handed the packet to him.

Emile returned his salute and accepted the packet. "Thanks soldier. Mail is always welcome."

"Yes, Sir," he replied and left.

There was an envelope on top of the bundle from Faye. He recognized her handwriting, and sat down at his field desk to open the letter. He had often written to her only to have the letters returned unopened. This letter from her gave him hope that she had forgiven him. His hands were shaking as he opened it to read:

April 30, 1944
Wells, Maine

Dear Father,

This packet of communications from the Army Medical Corps has been erroneously sent all over the world until it came to our home address in Berlin. Mother asked me to contact you. The next letter contains official notification of the death of Lieutenant Cora Lambert of the Nurse Corps. She was killed in a Japanese bombing raid on the island of Guadalcanal.

I knew that you were very close to her. Alpha told me that the last time I saw him. I'm so sorry for your loss, especially so soon after Alpha's untimely death. Evidently she had listed you as her next of kin and the notice got lost in the maze of this war until it came to Mother who was at the house in Berlin at that time. I told Mother that I wanted to be the one to tell you about Cora's death. I'm so sorry to be the bearer of such cruel news. May God forgive me! I know how this notice is going to affect you, Father. It's so unfair. I pray that God will be able to comfort you in this hour of loss. Alpha told me that she was a nurse and a wonderful lady who had captured your heart. I'm at a loss for words at such a heart-wrenching moment in your life.

I can't tell you how much it hurts for me to be the messenger of death at such a crucial moment in the war effort.

I apologize for my childish reaction to your response to my pregnancy. I hope that I've grown some since then. I love you, Father. You gave me the precious gift of a lifetime filled with warm memories of you. Forgive me, dear Father. Sending your letters back unopened was cruel and uncalled for. How I regretted those foolish actions!

Forgive me,

Your daughter,

Faye

The letter from Faye was a welcome offer of reconciliation that pleased him, but the dark message about Cora devastated him emotionally and physically. Anger, grief, and shock hit him, all at the same time. He collapsed on the cot and wept uncontrollably. The sudden news drained the energy from his body. The gentle nurse was lost to him and to all of the wounded soldiers she cared for. It was not fair... He cried until there were no more tears to shed. He laid partially comatose on the cot for a long time until a young platoon leader, Lieutenant Farnsworth, called to see if he was prepared to get in the chow line for supper. He saw him lying on the cot and kneeled beside him.

"What's wrong, Colonel? Do you want me to call for a medic or a doctor?"

Emile heard the young officer and was slow to respond. That worried the Lieutenant. "Sir, can you hear me?"

"Yes, I hear you. Lieutenant," Emile sat up on the edge of the cot. "I'll be okay. News from home got me off balance for a while. Go ahead, Lieutenant. I'll be along shortly."

"I'm starved; those cliffs at Wight are keeping us busy," Lieutenant Farnsworth exclaimed before leaving the tent.

Emile sprinkled water from his canteen on his face and wiped himself dry. He quickly checked what was left in the packet of mail. The original notification of Cora's death was on top and he read it. She had been killed right after the last letter she wrote to him. He had wondered why he had not heard from her since. It had been several months.

He stood up and combed his hair. It was important for him to put his personal grief and feelings to one side. Right now he was about to command the most difficult mission he had ever had in the Army. Many lives depended on his judgment. His men deserved his best effort, and personal things had to be put aside. He left the tent and waited for the enlisted men to go through the chow line first. Officers always followed the men. Some officers didn't like it, but Emile was firm with his decision. That had been one of his first orders for the Ranger battalion, and it was a good way to show the men how much the officers valued their service. Living in the same quarters also helped to bring the battalion into a cohesive family brotherhood. They fought together, and they lived together. It was a simple adjustment to make, and it made the unit more manageable in combat.

After the evening meal, Emile called a special meeting of the three companies. They quickly gathered around him beneath the mess tent, anxious to hear what he had for news. The three companies contained 225 men who would soon be engaged in one of the most daring and dangerous missions of the war. He wanted them to know how important their mission was for the successful invasion of Europe. The sun was setting behind the white cliffs on the English shoreline as they gathered around Emile. He looked at the men and was proud of them. They represented a typical cross section of the American population. They faced an almost impossible mission with faith, courage, and determination.

He climbed on top of a table and held his hands up for the officers to gather close to him. "Rangers, "he began, "I want to announce that the day we've been training for has been determined. June 5th is attack day, weather permitting. We'll attack and climb the cliffs at Point du Hoc, strategically located between Omaha and Utah beaches. We are to precede the main invasion force by several hours so that we can silence the large cannons on top of the cliffs. There will be no more training exercises. I want all of you to write home and rest until we load the transport for France. You'll be isolated from the rest of the world until we pull anchor to leave England.

"I'm privileged to command such a fine body of men. You can't write home about it now, but you'll be able to tell your children and grandchildren what will take place on the shore of France as we assault the cliffs. We have been as well prepared for this mission as humanly possible. Before we board the transport you will be given brand new Thompson sub-machine guns. I insisted that they be issued for this mission. At that time you'll also be issued ammo for the Thompsons, conventional grenades, thermite grenades to disable the German cannons, and water and ration packs.

"We'll be supported by an American and a British destroyer, and a U.S. Coast Guard cutter with a shallower draft, capable of getting closer to the beach where it will support us during the climb of the cliff. The cutter has installed two new quad-fifty-caliber machine guns on its forward deck specifically for cover while we're busy climbing the cliffs. They deserve special thanks for their dedication to our mission.

"I have one last thing to say. If any man feels that he cannot complete this mission, for whatever reason, he should notify his platoon leader, and his request will be accepted without question."

Emile paused for that statement to register and continued, "Do you have any questions?"

The group was silent until a corporal in the front row held up his hand. "Yes, Corporal." Emile acknowledged him.

"Colonel, I've been selected by my buddies to act as a spokesperson for the group. It has been a unique experience to serve under your command during the grueling, difficult days of training and development of skills needed for this mission. We know how much responsibility you carry on your shoulders, and we want you to know that when we scale those cliffs on D-Day, the Germans will soon learn that they are up against the first team. We'll take those cliffs and silence the cannons prior to the invasion. Wherever you lead us, we'll follow with pride and respect. Thank you, Sir, for your confidence in us. You will not be disappointed."

Emile had a hard time controlling his emotions. Tears formed in his eyes as he scanned the young soldiers he was about to order on a most difficult mission. Yes, he thought: "These men are the first team." He jumped off the table and exited the tent.

Returning to the privacy of his tent, Emile was overcome with emotion. The young corporal had hit a sensitive nerve that touched him. The brutal fact that some of his buddies would not survive the attack was enough to rattle any man with a conscience. He loved every man in his command. They had suffered under the most demanding training exercises Emile had ever witnessed, and there wasn't a bad apple in the bunch! His pride in them was tempered by the reality that he would soon have to sign the letters that would be sent home to loved ones. The cruel words: "We are saddened to inform you..." would change a family forever.

He knew how it would hurt. The news of Cora's death had destroyed all of his dreams and hopes for the future. He sat in a chair and held his head in his two hands and wept. The tears were not for him alone. A vision of Cora as she proudly sat in the Chevy coupe when he first saw her contained the tears. A smile crossed his lips. That memory was permanently engraved in his psyche. Proud, gracious, and gentle, Cora was the embodiment of everything that was right in the world. When he was with her, a feeling of peace and contentment filled his heart. Now she was gone!

The period of extreme grief was beginning to worry Emile. He was responsible for the most demanding mission of the European campaign, and he was going to need all of his mental and physical resources if it was to be accomplished. The men deserved his best efforts…

Chapter Twenty-One

The cliffs of Point du Hoc sit astride Omaha and Utah Beaches like a large dagger into the English Channel. Dark and ominous, they are an elevated section of the French coastline that dominates the area. The Allied Command that planned the massive invasion of Fortress Europe were concerned that the six large-caliber coastal cannons built on top of the Point could wreak havoc with the invasion force. The cannons were capable of sinking ships ten miles out to sea, and could thwart the entire operation before the Allies touched the beaches. General Eisenhower insisted that "elimination of the guns on Point du Hoc were an absolute must prior to the invasion."

Bombers had been launched to saturate topside with bombs while the battleship USS Texas had stood miles out to sea and bombarded the Point with its large-caliber cannons. To insure that the guns were positively silenced, the Rangers were assigned the mission of doing so, regardless of cost, before the planned invasion. Failure to do so would cancel the invasion.

Emile and his team were fully aware of the significance of their mission. He was also concerned about the potential for large casualties for his beloved Rangers. He was more proud than ever when not a single man asked to be relieved. The history books would portray their courage, tenacity, and willingness to sacrifice their all for a just cause. Emile was leading the best!

The Rangers boarded a large English transport and were prepared to get underway when the operation was cancelled for the day. The Rangers took advantage of the delay to double check their weapons, and to again review the sequences of their attack. Every man knew the drill by heart. Regardless of losses, they were to continue the climb up the cliffs until they were able to reach the top. Emile informed the men that he would be the first man to climb one of the ropes. Once they reached the top, it was crucial that they quickly establish a defensive line with as many men as possible and push inland to the casements of the artillery pieces that seriously threatened the invasion force that was an hour behind their efforts. Failure to silence the guns was not an option. Regardless of cost, that objective had to be completed! Every man carried thermite grenades. They were a silent weapon consisting of a mixture of aluminum powder and a metal oxide that produced extremely high heat capable of melting heavy metals.

Emile again reviewed the plan with the men and then went to his bunk to write a letter to Faye. He suggested that the men do the same and to turn their letters into the mail boxes on the ship.

Somewhere in England

June 5, 1944

My Dear Daughter,

I can't tell you where I am or what I'm doing, however, I want to tell you again, I love you. I'm so sorry that I gave you pause to doubt that fact.

The men are quiet tonight. That is typical when they are about to enter combat. There's a real chance that this could be my last letter to you, Faye. If that is the case, I'll be joined by your brother, Alpha, and we'll celebrate our reunion in Heaven.

During the course of my life, I've been stubborn about my career in the Army. You children and your mother had to bear long absences and frequent moves that are a normal part of a career-soldier's life. I always knew how difficult those times were for all of you. I hope and pray that I leave a legacy you'll all be proud of if it is my time to be called home. If that is the case, do not mourn my loss. Remember the good times we shared. I'll write to your mother tonight. We've had our differences over the years, but you should know that she loves you very much.

It's important for me to tell you how honored I am to command the best trained and dedicated soldiers this country has ever produced. If we accomplish our assigned mission, you'll probably read about it shortly after the fact. We pray for success. I love you more than you'll ever know.

Dad

The large transport weighed anchor at midnight to take its place as the vanguard of the invasion of Fortress Europe. That evening, General Eisenhower gave the order to "go." The plan was for the Rangers to be deposited at the base of the cliffs on Point du Hoc an hour prior to the main invasion. It was pitch dark when they transferred from the transport to the British landing craft several miles out to sea from the coast. The seas were boiling and rough. The Rangers had a difficult time making the transfer to the landing craft.

The battleship *USS Texas* began to bombard the Point with its heavy artillery cannons while the landing crafts were carrying the Rangers to shore. They lost several landing crafts in the rough seas. The Coast Guard cutter and two destroyers accompanied the Rangers to the shoreline. The landing crafts had miscalculated the original landing area and deposited them to the east of the original. That placed them behind schedule, and they had to fight their way to the west under heavy machine gun fire. Losses were heavy. Emile called the backup fire control officers to give him maximum fire support prior to their attempt to climb the cliffs. He was alarmed at the heavy losses they had already sustained and was doubtful if he had enough men to carry out their mission. He went ashore with 225 Rangers. A backup force of 500 Rangers was ordered to land on Omaha Beach and fight their way overland to the top of Point du Hoc to reinforce Emile's initial assault team.

Once they arrived at the base of the cliffs, they had outfitted one of the landing crafts with an aerial ladder from the London Fire Department, but had to abandon it because they could not get close enough to the base of the cliffs. Mortars were used to shoot grapples, with ropes attached, to the top of the cliffs. Some of these ropes were made into ladders that made them easier to climb. Several did not hold the weight of a man and they fell to the ground. Emile placed his Thompson sub-machine gun over his shoulder, grasped a single rope, and began to shimmy up the cliff. The destroyers and Coast Guard cutter were giving him maximum support. They saturated the hilltop with lead and were prepared to lift the barrage as the Rangers climbed the cliffs. The Germans were throwing hand grenades, rocks, even garbage, over the edge of the cliff. A grenade bounced off Emile's helmet and exploded below him, killing several Rangers climbing the ropes. Others rapidly took their place. It took Emile only fifteen minutes to reach the top where he hugged the ground and called for more support while he organized a defense line slightly over the edge of the cliffs. The plateau was relatively flat and very few enemy soldiers were visible. They were carefully concealed behind concrete casements, yet they maintained a murderous rate of fire against the Rangers.

Many men were lost trying to climb the ladders. The few that made it to the top experienced even more deadly fire from the Germans. Every Ranger forming Emile's defense line was returning fire as rapidly as possible. More and more men, exhausted from the climb, joined them. Now they had enough force to attack inland to locate the cannons. Time was running out! The invasion fleet was nearing the invasion beaches! The quad-fifty caliber machine guns on the cutter were especially effective in holding the Germans from overrunning their small foothold at the edge of the plateau on top of the hill.

The small line of Rangers pushed recklessly inland to get closer to their destination – the coastal cannons. They lost a lot of men making that push inland. Emile and a small group of Rangers had located the gun casements. Something was wrong! The casements had telephone poles to look like gun barrels from the air. They had been deceived by the wily Germans! He called his central control to notify them that he was working his way to the coastal road that ran along the Normandy beaches. The fast charging Rangers advanced inland about a half mile to the road where they set up a roadblock to stop any German threat to their positions. Emile again called central control giving them the necessary coordinates, asking for maximum artillery support.

He then took several of his Rangers to investigate marks of heavy-tracked vehicles heading into a large orchard. Among the trees, covered with camouflage netting, he found the six large guns of Point du Hoc. Surprisingly, the guns were not manned! Large numbers of Germans could be heard in a nearby mess hall. Quickly, Emile and the Rangers methodically began to dismantle the weapons, and threw silent thermite grenades into the breech mechanisms. They ignited without a sound and immediately began to melt the heavy metal. Black clouds of smoke rose from the mounts. That startled the German crews, and they emptied the hall determined to make the Americans pay a price for their success. It was an intense engagement, and Emile was afraid that he could not hold his ground against the onslaught.

He called central command again to inform them that the guns had been silenced, but he was in danger of being overrun unless he had reinforcements immediately. He came ashore with 225 Rangers. He and his aide estimated that they had 80 to 90 men capable of holding the line. All day they held the thin line on the roadway and were slowly losing men! Emile was more than concerned; he was in danger of being wiped out by the large number of German soldiers on top of the Point. Towards evening, a platoon of Rangers had fought across Omaha Beach and had pushed their way to the roadway on top of the Point. The relief column probably saved Emile's shrinking defense line. The larger contingent of men repeatedly stopped the desperate German charges. All night the two sides battled each other to the point of total exhaustion. The Rangers were not relieved until two days later.

Emile's elite Ranger unit had lost 75 percent of its men. Trucks were available for them to ride down to the beach. Their wounded had already been moved to the necessary medical units on the beach below. It was an exhausted group of Rangers who handed over Point du Hoc to their replacements. They were unaware that they had created a legacy of courage and heroism that would long be remembered.

On the way down from the promontory, the column of trucks was attacked by several German tanks. They had hit two of the trucks before the American tanks guarding the column could give return fire. Emile was in the first truck that was hit with a large-caliber weapon that threw the men out of the body of the truck. The German tanks were quickly dispatched and everyone turned to check on the men. Two were killed and several wounded, including Emile. The wounded were rushed to the nearest mobile hospital unit on the beachhead.

The Rangers were concerned about Emile. He was covered with blood and his left arm was hanging down over the edge of the stretcher held only by a few strands of muscle. They followed him into the large tent. The attending doctor immediately ordered blood plasma. He was bleeding profusely! The exhausted Rangers, grimy and sweaty from days of intense combat, silently stood around his ravaged body. The doctor saw how much the patient meant to them.

"Men," he announced in a soft voice, looking at the weary soldiers. "Your commander is in God's hands now. We'll do the best we can, but he's going to need all the prayers you can offer for him."

A burly sergeant wiped a tear from his soiled cheek and said, "He's a very special man, Sir. We could never have done it without him leading the way."

The kind doctor embraced the Ranger. "We're proud of all of you who scaled those terrible cliffs! We'll do our best for the Colonel, Sergeant."

The Rangers held a 24-hour vigil at the hospital facility on the beach following the treatment of their Colonel. Only after they had received word that he was going to survive the massive wounds did they seek the rest and food they desperately needed.

Chapter Twenty Two

A month later, across the dark Atlantic Ocean, Bonnie had just received the last letter Emile wrote the evening before D-Day.

She had been notified of his wounds and that he was being treated in an Army hospital in England long before she got his letter. She took out his letter and quietly read it again:

Somewhere in England

June 5, 1944

Dear Bonnie,

I just finished writing a note to Faye, hoping that she forgives me for the hurtful statement I blurted out in anger at her. I've always loved that girl and I never thought that she was any person other than my own flesh and blood. You must know that is true. When she was born I forgave you and I never felt any different towards her than I did for Alpha. That is a truthful statement.

Just the mention of our son's name brings back happy memories and an ache in my heart that never ends. How I miss that boy! I'm a soldier who has seen death on a large scale, yet our son's death still hurts.

I also confess that I'm having a hard time accepting the death of Cora, a gentle nurse who was a joy to be with. Her gracious and gentle ways touched a part of me that is hard to let go… I apologize for my rambling about things in the past. I knew that your marriage to Lewis was not as good as the two of you pretended. I can truthfully tell you that those few days you visited me at the hospital in Washington were good for me. Thanks for helping me with my breakup with Faye.

Tonight is the eve of an important combat mission for my Ranger team. I apologize if I seem a little somber tonight. That often happens in a soldier's life. This battle is one in which we have been training hard and long to accomplish. I told Faye and I will tell you that there's a good chance that this will be my last letter to you. Don't be burdened by that statement. I've been preparing a long time for any mission assigned to me and I accept the risks associated with being a soldier who follows orders.

If that prophecy becomes a reality, I want you to know that I apologize for being primarily responsible for our failed marriage. I've been thinking that maybe there was a chance for us to rekindle what we once had in the early years of our marriage. Think about it, Bonnie, and let me know your thoughts. I wish you the best across the wide Atlantic.

Sincerely,

Emile

Bonnie read the telegram again and placed it on the kitchen table. The radio was playing a song that had touched the hearts of every family in the country who had a loved one overseas. Vera Lynn, an English singer, was singing, *The White Cliffs of Dover*. It brought tears to Bonnie's eyes, and she wept softly, staring at an old photo of Emile when he was a Captain. A cry of despair pierced her lips as she laid her head in her arms on the table and wept.

She had been praying a long time for an opportunity to make amends for all the times she failed to support her Emile. The thoughts that he wrote gladdened her heart, and she silently thanked God that she might have a chance to make him happy. He truly deserved that. Once again he was lying in a hospital beyond her reach. She felt helpless and gently folded his letter and the telegram, placing them on the table.

Later that evening, Bonnie called Faye in Wells, Maine, to let her know that her father had been seriously wounded. Faye answered the phone. "Hello."

"Faye, this is your mother. I just received a telegram from the War Department that your father has been seriously wounded and is in a hospital near London. The telegram did not elaborate on the seriousness of his wounds. We'll pray that he will recover as he usually does."

"Mom, I've been following news on the D-Day invasion and read a report in a magazine about a group of Army Rangers that climbed steep cliffs to destroy enemy installations prior to the main invasion at Normandy. Their losses were high, but they accomplished their mission. I had a feeling that was Dad's outfit. It would be something that the Rangers do, and I bet he was their commander for the mission," Faye was excited and proud.

"You may be right, Faye," Bonnie said in a soft tone. "His Medal of Honor tells the world how brave he is. I'm so proud of him and pray that he'll be coming home to us soon."

Faye heard what her mother told her and wondered if there might be a chance for a reconciliation. "Would you marry Dad again, Mom?"

The question did not surprise Bonnie. "I pray for a chance to make amends for the way I treated your father for so many years. He hinted about such a possibility in his last letter to me. He deserves better than I gave him. I can admit that now. The lady, Cora, would have been good for him, but now she's gone. Pray for us, Faye. I really want that chance to make him happy again."

"I'd like to see that happen too, Mother. Alpha was hoping that it might be possible for you two. Thanks for calling, Mother. I'll write Dad tonight. I've been stubborn and difficult when I should have been more supportive of him. Goodnight, Mother"

"Goodnight, Faye. I love you."

Faye hung up and sat quietly watching the restless sea out the window of her small apartment at the beach. Her father had once again placed his life on the line in defense of freedom. The ocean separated them by many miles, but she was with her Dad in spirit in this desperate hour of need. She prayed for his recovery, and she asked for forgiveness for her stubborn dismissal of him when he needed her support and love more than ever. Her mother had been more reflective and sober than usual tonight over the phone. How nice it would be if they could come together again!

She sat to write the letter to her father so that she could mail it on her way to catch the bus for Portland where she was attending an educational seminar that was required to keep her teaching certificate. She was happy teaching the first grade in Wells.

In the meantime, across the Atlantic, her father was struggling to stay alive. He had survived the rapid rush to the hospital on Omaha Beach, thanks to the quick action of an Army medic who was able to give him the life-saving blood plasma. He had been bleeding a lot. That act by the young medic saved Emile's life. Once he was in the field hospital, the surgeons immediately amputated the shattered remains of his left arm, leaving a short stub several inches above the elbow. They cauterized the wound to stop the bleeding and dressed the remaining arm with tight compress bandages.

Emile's condition warranted the facilities of a hospital with better equipment and personnel to handle his severely injured body, so he was stabilized and sent via a rapid-shuttle-craft back to England. The team of American surgeons at the Army hospital near London were prepared to receive him.

They stabilized Emile and had surgically removed all of the metal fragments in his body. One week later, they met in a conference room to review his case. The chief surgeon read all of the daily ward logs since he was transferred from Omaha Beach. "This is a courageous soldier that has already won the Medal of Honor in Sicily. He has lost his left arm, but I believe that there is enough of a stub to attach an artificial arm once the upper arm has healed properly.

"However, loss of an arm is not the Colonel's only problem. We also removed his spleen, and had to surgically remove a portion of his lungs and about half of his stomach. He's going to require the services of a good internal medicine physician until his body acclimates itself to the drastic invasion to his body. He's lucky to be alive. There is also a problem with his left leg. One piece of shrapnel that we had removed from his spine had partially severed nerves that control the movements of his leg. At this stage of recovery, I am doubtful that he will have full use of his left leg. Does anyone have anything to add?"

A young Army captain suggested that the patient be transferred to the states as soon as possible. "The Colonel has been under so much sedation during and after numerous operations that he has had little time to become aware of his limitations. The value of familiar faces and surroundings is invaluable for his recovery."

The team agreed with the proposal as soon as he was at a stable condition and was able to communicate with them. One of the nurses was able to carry on a conversation with Emile a few days after the conference. She told him about the decision to send him home by aircraft and asked him where he wanted to go. He had quickly answered anywhere in New England. When he was told the truth about his loss of an arm and the unknown condition of his left leg, he became morbid and discouraged and withdrew from further conversation. It was a normal reaction when a patient faces the truth about their limitations. Frequently soldiers showed more courage and bravery in the hospital wards than they did on the battlefield.

Mid-June, 1944, he was flown to Boston Army Hospital. The day after his arrival, he was given a thorough check of his condition. He was able to have visitors, and Faye and Bonnie were told that they could visit with him for a short period of time. Seeing his family was an important part of the healing process. He was very weak during the initial visit. He was being fed intravenously until his body was able to digest food. He still had a lot of discomfort in his stomach. The battlefield wounds and the invasive surgery were going to take a long period of time to heal properly. Right now he had the task of rebuilding his body to accommodate the destructive power of jagged steel against soft human tissue.

He did recognize Faye and Bonnie on that first visit. They were shocked when they saw him. The man lying in the hospital bed was a far cry from the robust person they had sent off to war. The terror of his experiences showed in his eyes. They were frightened with his hollow stare. As soon as he recognized them he began to cry. It was difficult for him to talk, and that embarrassed him. They left the ward after whispering in his ear that they would be seeing him every day.

That night, Faye and Bonnie returned to their hotel room filled with apprehension and concern. Faye was unable to contain the tears that ran down her cheeks. This time, her father had been ravaged by the terror of war, and it hurt because there was nothing they could do about it. He was truly in God's hands! They both prayed for his recovery, knowing that it was going to take a long, long time.

Bonnie was able to hide her tears. More than ever she was angry at herself for leaving Emile for another man! She prayed not only for his recovery, but for the opportunity to care for him and show him how much she loved him. In the past, she had failed him and the children and regretted it, knowing that she did not deserve the privilege of once again being his wife.

Faye saw how her mother reacted to her father's condition and asked a question that had been on her mind ever since her father's stay at the Walter Reed Hospital several months ago. "Mother, if you had a chance would you marry dad again?"

Bonnie looked at Faye through tear-dimmed eyes and replied, "You don't beat about the bush, do you, young lady?"

"I'm not trying to pry. It's just that I've never seen you as attentive to father as you've been today and at the hospital in Washington."

"Well, Honey, your father has had to handle the loss of our son, the loss of a lady that he loved, and now he has come home from the war with wounds that will limit him for the rest of his life. My God, how much punishment can a human being take? He needs and has earned our support. The answer to your question is yes. I would be honored to be his wife again!"

"I knew it, Mom." Faye reached out to hug her.

"I'm staying in Boston until he's able to come home," Bonnie cried in Faye's arms. "I knew that I was hurting your father when I left him for Lewis. I was selfish and regretted that part of my life more than I can explain. I'd like to think that I've grown some since then. Oh, I disappointed your father so often in the past. I wouldn't be surprised if he pushed me away. I deserve that."

That evening, Bonnie sat and looked out the window and watched a full moon rise out of the East, casting bright rays through the window. She looked upon it as a good omen for the future. She hoped that it was shining in Emile's room at the same time. He was near a window with a view of Boston Harbor. He always liked to watch the moon and the sun as they rose and fell across the universe. He was a gentle man who was pleased by simple things in life. She had not always appreciated those traits or his love of country. Now, she could readily admit that she had been selfish and self-centered.

Emile's recovery began that first day in Boston when he had a visit from his family. He had already accepted the limitations and the reality of his physical condition. It was going to take some time. The fact that a large percentage of his battalion was killed, capturing the cliffs at Normandy was an adjustment he found difficult to accept. At least he was alive! So many were not...

Whenever Faye and Bonnie came for a visit, they volunteered to massage his legs so that he would not lose the muscular ability to move them. He still did not have any feeling in his left leg and was unable to move it. That did not deter Bonnie or Faye from keeping the muscular tone from disintegrating. If and when the nerves rejoined, he needed the muscles to move his leg and, hopefully, to walk!

Fay had to return to York, Maine, to teach school the last of August. She left her father in better spirits than she saw on that first visit. She promised him that she would be back as often as possible and embraced him. Tears filled their eyes.

"I love you, Dad."

"I love you too, Honey. I'm a grateful dad. How lucky I am!"

Bonnie continued to come to the hospital every day after Faye left. She not only attended to Emile's every need, she helped the other veterans in the ward. She fed some who could not do it for themselves and wrote letters for those who asked her to do so. One day she was helping a soldier at the far end of the ward finish his lunch. She looked at the chart on a clipboard at the foot of the bed and learned that it was Major Tom Huntley, Emile's executive officer of the Ranger battalion. He had been seriously wounded while climbing a rope up the cliffs at Point du Hoc when he caught a German hand grenade and tried to throw it back up the cliffs when it exploded in his hand. He fell fifty feet to the rocks at the base of the cliffs. He broke a number of bones in his body and lost his right hand. Bonnie was quick to have the orderlies move Major Huntley's bed next to Emile. It was good therapy for the two officers to be able to talk about what happened to them. She learned that he was from Massachusetts, and his wife, Karen, visited him every day.

That next day, Karen brought their daughter, Angela, to see her dad. She was a cute three-year-old with coal black hair cut short below her ears with bangs that covered apart of her forehead. She apprehensively hugged her daddy while Mother held her so as not to disturb the intravenous tube in his arm. "Mommy told me to be good. I love you, Daddy."

She reminded Emile of the times when he and Faye had gone to the beach to build sand castles. He enjoyed Angela's visits almost as much as Tom did.

She soon became restless, and Karen got ready to leave the hospital. She held Angela so that she could kiss her daddy good-bye. She then reached up to take Emile's right hand in hers and said, "Good-bye, Mr. Ranta. Mommy takes me home now." She waved to the two soldiers as she disappeared from the ward.

Chapter Twenty Three

Christmas came quickly for the patients at the Boston Army Hospital. In the few months since Emile and Tom had been transferred from England, they both improved better than anticipated. The stub of Emile's arm had healed enough so that the administration designed an artificial arm specifically for him and attached it. Then began long and tedious hours of practicing to develop the muscular system in his shoulders and arm.

He was able to take soft foods such as "Jello," ice cream and soups heavy in broth in small doses several times a day. This routine was designed to develop and to normalize his digestive system. The one thing that he craved the most was coffee. He was addicted to coffee all during his long tenure in the Army. His persona and attitude changed when he was able to have an occasional half cup of coffee. Foods that contained a lot of acid, such as citrus fruit and tomatoes, irritated his stomach; thus they were temporarily avoided. In time he might be able to digest small amounts of those kinds of foods. He took a few Tums each day to counter the acid in his stomach.

The hospital administration worked diligently to make Christmas, 1944, a day of joy and hope for the future. Every patient in the facility responded positively to the atmosphere in the wards. Faye and Bonnie joined Tom's wife, Karen, and daughter, Angela, in the festivities at the ward. Christmas music was piped through the hospital's sound system to every room. It had been a good day for patients and guests. Flowers were popular gifts, and the wards were filled with the soft fragrance of roses and geraniums. Karen had brought Tom a large heliotrope flower. Its aroma spread throughout the ward. Everyone remarked how striking the blood-red color was.

Bonnie and Faye witnessed how Emile had responded to the festivities of the day. He was making progress, and they were proud of his positive attitude. Towards the afternoon, Emile and many of the patients were getting tired, so Karen held little Angela for her to kiss her father good-bye.

Placing Angela on the floor, she turned to Bonnie and said, "I know that hotel rooms are hard to get in the city proper. Would you like to come to our home at Gloucester? I'll be coming back to the hospital in the morning to be with Tom. We have a guest room and would be glad to share it with you."

"That sounds like a great idea, Karen," Tom replied.

Bonnie turned to Faye. "What do you think, Faye?"

"We had not made any provisions for an overnight stay," she replied. "It would be nice to spend another day with father. Thanks for the offer, Karen. It's generous of you."

Emile had closed his eyes and seemed to be sleeping soundly. Bonnie left a note telling him they would be back in the morning. They left the facility with Karen and Angela.

Karen waved to Tom as they left the ward.

Tom and Karen lived in a small Cape Cod home on the coast in Gloucester, Mass. They rode in their 1940 Ford sedan. Karen told Bonnie and Faye that the government issued them a coupon so that they could purchase as much gasoline as was needed to see her husband in the hospital, thirty miles from home. That Christmas the ground was free of snow, but the cold had been quite severe. Warm clothing always felt good.

Bonnie always enjoyed the seacoast. Most of her life she had spent in the mountainous regions of New England. She especially liked the brisk air that generated a healthy appetite and a sound sleep at nighttime.

Angela had fallen asleep in Bonnie's arms for most of the trip. As soon as they arrived, Karen showed Bonnie and Faye their guest room and excused herself to put Angela to bed for the night. All of the excitement at the hospital had made her tired. Later that evening over hot cocoa and toast, Bonnie and Karen sat in the kitchen and talked about their lives. Bonnie was quick to inform Karen that she and Emile were not married.

Karen was surprised. "I never would have thought that, Bonnie. You two seemed so comfortable with each other. It's nice that Emile and Tom are sharing the same ward in the hospital. They'll help each other. Tom's wounds are not as severe as Emile's. The doctor told me that his broken bones should heal in time, and he'll be able to walk and move about without any limitations. I'm so thankful for that. I note that Emile is determined to not let his wounds restrict him from getting on with his life. I admire that kind of courage and determination. Your presence at the hospital will help him climb that mountain."

Bonnie was close to tears when she answered Karen. "I can confide with you that I pray every day for the chance to be his wife once again. I look back on those years when he had decided to make a career out of the Army. I was very much opposed to the way the Army interfered in the lives of its members, and I selfishly triggered our divorce to get away from the rigid control. It's true that families of all the career servicemen have more problems than the civilian population."

Karen finished her cocoa and said, "I understand that many career men had family problems."

"I hope that I've matured since then. I regret my selfishness and am thankful for the opportunity to be with him while he struggles to overcome horrendous wounds. I envy what you and Tom have," Bonnie admitted.

Faye had been an interested listener to the conversation. She silently studied her mother while she confessed that she was wrong to leave her father. That evening Faye saw a different person talk about her shortcomings to a near stranger and agreed with what her mother was telling Karen. Over the years, neither of her parents ever spoke unkindly of each other. If they had harbored bitterness, they kept it to themselves. Faye and Alpha both knew that they were loved by both of their parents.

"I don't know about you two, but I'm exhausted," Karen admitted to her guests. "I hope you two are comfortable in the room. "I'll keep Angela quiet so that you two can rest if she wakes up in the evening." Karen turned to Faye and asked, "What do you do for work, Faye?"

"I'm a teacher at Wells, Maine," Faye replied. "Mother and I appreciate your hospitality. Rooms are scarce in the city."

Bonnie embraced Karen. "Thanks, Karen. I'm ready to retire, too."

"I'll set up the coffee pot. Whoever gets up first can turn it on." Karen pointed to the percolator on the range. "Tom is a heavy coffee drinker, and I've become one since he's been away."

"Emile is an addict, too," Bonnie replied. "It seems to be an Army tradition."

"Dad got all of us hooked on the stuff," Faye added, embracing Karen. "You've turned this house into a home, Karen. The peaceful energy that is present here is a reflection of the devotion you and Tom share."

That night, Bonnie lay on the bed closer to the window with a view of the ocean and watched the moon shine on the water. She thought of Emile and silently prayed for his recovery and for the chance to be his wife once again. She and Emile never had the trust and easy-going relationship that Tom and Karen enjoyed. It had touched her heart. Throughout the years with Emile, there was always an unspoken indifference that made them both unhappy. They had simply lived together. Emile was committed to an ideal greater than himself while she was often engulfed in her own selfish outlook on life!

The next day, Karen drove Bonnie and Faye to the hospital. "Tell Tom that I'll be in to see him later in the day. I need to run some errands and go shopping this morning. It was nice having you two as guests."

"Thanks for being so helpful, Karen," Bonnie told her.

Faye reached through the window of the car and shook Karen's hand. "I've enjoyed your hospitality, Karen. Over the years I've always been impressed by the fraternal relationships that exist between members of Army families. I hope to see you again soon."

"I, too, enjoyed the company," Karen replied.

They found Emile sleeping soundly, and they quietly went to the waiting room on the ward's floor. Faye informed her mother that she had to leave on the morning bus to Maine. She was conducting a seminar on the school's curriculum and needed some time to prepare the subject material. She was leaving Boston in a better frame of mind: her father was improving every day both mentally and physically, and that pleased her. She was also hoping that her absence would give her mother and father a chance to be alone. Perhaps, the hopes and dreams that her mother harbored could become reality…

Faye left the waiting room and checked in on her father one last time. He was awake, and a nurse was bringing him his breakfast. Her father saw her enter the ward and smiled at her. She told him that she had to leave.

Emile reached out for her with his right hand. "I can't tell you how much your visit has meant to me, Faye. You've always had a very special place in my heart, and I'm so proud of the young lady you've become. The children in your class are lucky kids. I love you, Honey. I always have."

"I know that, Dad," she kissed him good-bye on the forehead. "I'll keep in touch on the week-ends."

Bonnie had witnessed their exchange and was moved by the depth of their feelings for each other. "Goodbye, Faye. I'll keep you informed of your Father's progress."

They watched her leave the ward. She paused at the door and waved, sending him a big smile.

"She's turned out to be a lovely young lady," Bonnie remarked, kissing Emile on the cheek.

"I'm thankful that our breakup has been forgotten," Emile said, moving his left arm in a circle. "I need to exercise the arm more now that they've developed a tong on the end of my new arm. I told the physical therapist that I'd like to try a caliper device for the end of my arm instead of a hook. He told me that it would only be usable when I move my arm against my body to activate a set of claws… Then he suggested that I try a hook because I would become versatile quicker with that than with a claw."

Bonnie saw Emile's enthusiasm and willingness to explore different things during his rehabilitation at the Boston hospital. "Have they told you when you might be able to go home to Berlin?"

"They said it was up to me, but they want to make certain that I'm proficient with the mechanized arm before they discharge me. My wounds are healing satisfactorily. The nurse said that it could be next month. It all depends on my left leg.

I've been able to feel something when the doctor pricks me with the needle. It even hurt a little bit. That was a few days ago."

"By then, snow will have to be plowed from the driveway," Bonnie mentioned.

"Yes, snow could be deep by then," Emile answered, sipping some of his coffee. "I might be able to plow the drive with a small tractor."

"You didn't tell me or Faye about your response to some form of stimuli. That must mean that the leg massaging must be working, Em. That's wonderful. I'm so proud of the way you've handled your situation. Faye will be glad to hear that. The nurse also told me that I could work on your leg this morning."

Emile was seeing a different Bonnie since he came to Boston. He had never seen her so concerned for his welfare. In the past, her attention was primarily for herself or to the children. He had often been hurt by her indifference to what he felt about things, and he had learned to live with that until the breakup.

"Do you think you could ever work as a forester, Em? I know it will depend on your leg's progress." She had been pleased with his positive attitude. It was a trait that he always had. She felt guilty that she had been so self-centered.

"We'll just have to wait it out and see what develops. Whatever it is, we have to accept it," he said, pleased with her show of support. He reached out for her. She grasped his right hand in her two and was unable to control the tears forming in her eyes. "You've been swell to me, Bonnie. I'm beginning to see the Bonnie that I fell in love with many years ago."

That simple statement encompassed her being with a warm glow of pure joy. Maybe her prayers were going to be fulfilled... maybe... She leaned over the bed and kissed him on the lips. It was a powerful moment that they would always cherish.

"Do we have a chance, Em? I was a fool to divorce you. Being here with you has given meaning to my life. I have a lot of making-up to do. The thought that I might accompany you to the little log cabin in Berlin has filled me with hope! For years my world has been filled with reproach and hatred for my actions. I lost you and I lost our son. The things I most loved were taken away from me..." She pulled away from Emile to wipe her eyes and to blow her nose. She felt weak and sat on the chair beside the bed.

Emile saw the depth of her despair and silently thanked his God. His Bonnie was offering them another chance! He placed his right hand on her shoulder and, in a voice filled with emotion, said, "Bonnie, I, too, have been thinking that we owe it to each other to give it another chance. I can't imagine returning to Berlin alone..."

Later that night, Bonnie sat alone in her hotel room looking out over Boston Harbor. The conversation that she and Emile had about a possible reconciliation had erased all of the uncertainties of the future. More than anything in the world, she wanted to be with Emile. The divorce that she had forced upon him was cruel and was a source of regret for a long time. Even after her marriage to Lewis Cohen, she often had feelings of loss that her new life could not fulfill. It was during this period of transition that she was able to honestly review the dreadful things she had done to Emile who suffered in silence.

She always put on the appearance of being happy when Alpha or Faye were around. It was a sham and she would not have been surprised if they saw through her deception. Bonnie knew that Emile had built the log Cabin in Berlin after their breakup. She had stayed there with Faye on several occasions. It was a warm, charming home that reflected Emile's love of simple things in life.

Before Bonnie left the ward, she had agreed with Emile that they would be married after he was discharged from the Army and had settled into the log cabin. Her home in Burlington, Vermont was placed on the market to be sold by a local realtor. She placed a low price on the property so as to sell it as quickly as possible. Soon the demand for homes would increase shortly after the war ended and the servicemen and women returned to civilian life.

Bonnie's tears that night were tears of joy, and she thanked her God for giving her the chance she feared was out of reach. Soon she would be Mrs. Bonnie Ranta again.

Chapter Twenty Four

The days after Emile and Bonnie made the decision to marry again passed quickly. There was a future to look forward to that fulfilled all their hopes and dreams. Emile's progress in the hospital was much improved. The staff was pleased with his positive outlook. Soon after he felt some response to a pin prick in his leg, Emile was able to move it slightly! The daily massages had maintained the tone of his leg muscles, and his response to stimuli pleased his staff of doctors and nurses. He would eventually gain full use of his leg! Bonnie and Emile celebrated their joy with a toast of champagne that Bonnie had purchased for the occasion. The doctors informed Emile that he could be discharged from the hospital on the very same day that the world was celebrating VE Day, May 8, 1945. The war in Europe was over! It had been a vicious and costly campaign. Now the Allies could concentrate on defeating the fanatical Japanese.

Emile, like most veterans of the costly campaign against the Germans, was relieved that it was over. The cost was high, and he still mourned for the young men he had lost while obtaining his final objective in France.

Tom had been discharged two weeks before VE Day. He returned alone to the hospital so that he could celebrate the victory with his fellow soldiers. It was a day of great festivity all over the world. Those individuals that still carried the scars from the war joined the celebration, and at the same time, they remembered those who were left buried in the soil of France.

Tom had been a courageous executive officer. He had won the respect and affection of the men who followed him up the ladder at Point du Hoc. Those who didn't make it to the top occupied a special place in his heart. Emile had similar feelings that he could not hide on this special occasion. Amid the shouts and cries that the guns were silent in Europe, there was a lot of tears shed for those who would remain forever young. Emile and Tom found it difficult to join the merriment that filled the hospital. Bonnie and Karen knew what their men were going through, and they remained close to their side for the day.

The VE Day celebration exhausted the veterans. Emile was still in a wheelchair until his leg muscles developed stronger. The doctors told him that in time he would be able to walk normally. He had to adapt to the situation and be a little more patient. He needed a little more time.

The weekend before Emile's discharge from the hospital, Bonnie and Faye used the Ford to go to Berlin to get the cabin ready for them to move in when he was released. They filled the gasoline tank with the special gas card issued to veterans. Faye had never seen her mother so relaxed and contented as she was making this trip through the beautiful White Mountains. She was coming back home and would be with her husband! During that trip to the log cabin, Faye had the feeling that Alpha's spirit was with them and that he, too, was experiencing the joy of the occasion. She shared her feelings with her mother and she admitted that she felt his presence when they first came through the door.

Bonnie and Emile had already planned a wedding ceremony by the local Methodist minister in Berlin. They both wanted a simple exchange of vows without any celebrations. They planned to celebrate the occasion together for the rest of their lives. Faye had been using the Ford while her father was in the hospital. When she was ready to leave Berlin after the wedding, her parents both agreed that she should have the vehicle. They had Bonnie's Nash Ambassador. It was a much more comfortable car for them.

"You know, Mother and Father," Faye said as she was leaving, "this has been one of the happiest days of my life. Seeing you two together is like a dream come true."

Emile embraced his daughter. "Thanks, dear lady, your unwavering support has been appreciated by both of us. Drive carefully through the mountains."

Bonnie embraced the two most important people in the world to her. "God has answered my prayers. My foolish heart was responsible for a lot of heartaches that the two of you had to endure. I'm going to make that up to both of you. With Em at my side, nothing is impossible. Thanks for always being there for us. We both love you very much, Faye."

It was a warm, teary-eyed goodbye as Em and Bonnie watched her leave the driveway with a wave and a honk of the horn.

A week after they were married, Emile received a letter from Cora's cousin who was responsible for settling her estate. The engagement ring that Emile had given to her was returned in the same letter. It also informed him that Cora had given him the 1932 Chevrolet coupe in her last will and testament. The little blue coupe with yellow wheels was currently being stored in Cora's barn. The cousin suggested that it be removed as quickly as possible.

Emile read the letter again and placed it on the kitchen table. His visions of Cora when he said good-bye to her brought tears to his eyes.

Bonnie had gone to the village to do some grocery shopping when the mail was delivered. She returned and found Emile distressed about something. "What's wrong, Em?" she asked, surprised that he did not meet her at the door to help carry the groceries in the way he always did.

He wanted to hide the tears and turned away from her, wiping his eyes and blowing his nose. He pointed to the letter on the table. She quickly picked it up and read it. They had been married for a short time and had not discussed the relationship he had with Cora. He had met Cora while they were still divorced, and she did not want to infringe upon things that were really none of her business. The depth of his distress worried her.

She placed the letter back on the table and wrapped her arms around his neck. "Emile, I knew about you and Cora. Alpha told me how you first met her on the road. At the time, I was pleased that you had found someone worthy of you. Do not think that your feelings for her have infringed upon our relationship, Em. If she brought some happiness and joy to your life, then she has my blessings. She must have been a wonderful lady to earn your affection, and it's only normal to mourn her passing. I'm a little jealous that I was not the one to make you happy, but it was my fault. I do not look upon her memory as competition for your affections. God took her and she is with the angels. Maybe Alpha is with her right now."

Emile turned to her and placed his arm and his mechanical arm around her. "Thank you for telling me that, Bonnie. Our relationship had not blossomed because the war years interfered. She was a very gracious soul who had not gotten over the love she had for her husband who was killed early in the war. I must say that you've matured into the same young lady I first married. Somewhere along the way we lost what we had those first years. I believe my Bonnie has found her way again. Hold me, Honey."

She kneeled and placed her head against his chest. "Whatever you decide to do about the ring and the Chevy coupe, I'll support you."

That evening, Emile contacted Cora's cousin and told him to donate the coupe to any family in their hometown that needed a vehicle. He promised the cousin that he would sell the ring and donate the proceeds to the Salvation Army. He felt that Cora would approve, and it made Bonnie proud of him. They had confronted a very private situation and resolved it without cross words or bad feelings. He was pleased with that accomplishment.

On August 14, 1945, the Town of Berlin exploded with bells ringing, horns blowing, people screaming for joy and fire engines sirens screaming. The Japanese had surrendered unconditionally to the Allies. The deadly war in the Pacific was over, and the killing and maiming of young bodies ceased. A thankful nation celebrated the news with uncontrollable joy and thanksgiving. Soon soldiers would be coming home to their families. Those who had perished would remain forever young, and they were mourned by loved ones who faced the future alone.

The celebration brought back memories of Alpha to Bonnie and Emile. He confided to Bonnie that he had been responsible for the death of hundreds of young men over the years while he served in the Army. Yet, the death of their son was something that he still had a hard time accepting. Emile and Bonnie prayed that evening for the ones who were not coming home to their families. It would leave an empty place in their hearts that only Alpha could fill. Tears fell in remembrance while they gave thanks that the war had ended. Faye had called to join them in prayer. The whole world celebrated the end of the vicious conflict that had shattered and affected almost every nation.

Bonnie had never lived in the log cabin, except when she visited Faye while Emile was overseas. She soon adapted to the smaller living quarters and was moved by its rustic charm. It had a warmth that her home in Vermont never attained. The renewed affection that she shared with Emile was partially responsible for her appreciation of their modest home. She desperately wanted it to be a home, not just a dwelling. Her determination to make this marriage work was made easy within the walls of the cabin. They began to attend church regularly, and she volunteered to help with the Sunday School lessons for children. It was a good opportunity to make new friends and to be a part of the community. Emile was proud of her.

That first winter they settled into the northern community and converted the cabin into a home filled with love and affection. After years of bloodshed and destruction, it was a welcome change. The world could look forward to the future without fear.

Emile had gained full use of his injured leg and had practiced faithfully with his mechanical arm so that he was capable of picking up small objects and holding a cup of coffee. One day he surprised Bonnie with a bouquet of roses and pinned one of them on her blouse with his artificial arm. It was a great achievement, and Bonnie was thrilled by his display of affection. Their relationship had blossomed into something special for both of them. The cabin was working its charm.

The job Emile had as a forester with the Brown Company was made available to him shortly after his move to Berlin. The company controlled several thousand acres of forestland that supplied the raw material for their paper production. He was responsible for the sustained production of pulpwood commensurate with the ability of the land to reproduce the annual cut of raw material. By the spring of 1946, Emile was promoted to general manager of the forest holdings with an increase in salary. While he was recovering from his wounds, he was frightened that he would not be able to make a living and take care of himself. When he married Bonnie, he was anxious to fill the role of provider for the family. The job gave him a sense of worth that was important to him.

Frequently on weekends, Bonnie and Emile would visit Tom and Karen at their home in Gloucester. During the winter months, Tom and Karen stayed at the cabin so that they could go skiing in the White Mountains, while little Angela stayed with Bonnie and Emile. Early one weekend in May, 1946, Bonnie and Emile had a desperate call from Tom and Karen. Her mother had passed away, and they wanted to visit Karen's family in Minnesota. They asked if it would be possible for them to drop off Angela at their home while they made the trip. It could be for several days. Bonnie had taken the call and was happy to have a chance to babysit little Angela. She asked Emile, and he heartily agreed. Tom told Bonnie that they could drop off Angela early the next morning. They expected to be gone about a week.

Chapter Twenty Five

The next day, Tom called Bonnie and Emile to let them know that they arrived in Minnesota and to check that everything was okay with Angela. The funeral for Karen's mother was the next day.

"Your lovely daughter is doing just fine, Tom," Bonnie told him. "She just ate a bowl of oatmeal and drank her orange juice. You two have done a wonderful job with her. Don't worry, we're hitting it off very well. Our prayers go out to you and Karen. Funerals can be exhausting, and they are never easy. When you return, you may find your daughter a little bit spoiled."

"I can't tell you when we'll be leaving, Bonnie. I hope Emile is doing well at his new job as a forester. I was proud to serve under him. He was a fine officer who had won the respect and affection of the men in his command. He deserves the best. I'll let you know when we're ready to leave, Bonnie. Thanks for everything."

"Thanks for calling, Tom. I'd let you speak to Angela, but she's in the bathtub right now," Bonnie told him.

"Give her our love, Bonnie."

Bonnie and Emile were amazed at how well little four-year-old Angela was starting to read and do her numbers. She was proud that she could spell her name. Emile took her with him to work on a day when he was going to inspect the logging camps north of Berlin that he could travel to in his company truck. He informed Bonnie that they would be back for supper. Angela was anxious to see the men cut down the trees. When Emile took her hand and led her down to the edge of a river she was a little afraid of the powerful horses that dragged the trees to the banks of the river.

They ate lunch at one of the camp's cook sheds. She was apprehensive at first with the burly woodsmen and their large beards, but she soon found that they were kind and gentle to her. They welcomed her to their noon meal. She enjoyed their favorite meal of the North Woods – baked beans and venison steak.

On the way home, Angela was tired and stretched out on the seat in the pickup truck laying her head on Emile's lap. He held her with his right hand so that she would not roll off the seat if he had to brake in a hurry. When he turned into their yard at home, she was fast asleep. He gently picked her up and carried her into the house. He smiled at her. She had enjoyed the day, but it had made her tired.

Bonnie had heard them turn into the driveway and opened the door for them. Emile look at her and cried aloud, "What's wrong, Bonnie?"

She saw that Angela was still asleep and motioned them into the bedroom. He gently laid her on the bed without waking her. Bonnie pulled a blanket over her, and quickly led Emile out of the room and closed the door.

"What is wrong, Bonnie?" he impatiently asked.

"Sit down, Em," she directed him to a chair. "I received a call this morning from Karen's cousin...."

"Yes, yes, Honey...what is it?"

"Tom and Karen have both been killed in an accident on the highway. A large truck hit their car broadside and killed both of them."

"My God....Are you sure, Bonnie?"

"Yes. Both died instantly at the scene. Evidently, the truck lost its brakes at an intersection and hit their car. Two other occupants in the car were seriously injured also."

"What are we going to do, Honey?" Emile sank into the chair. "How can we tell little Angela that she's an orphan?"

They called the number that Tom had given them when they left for Kansas. There was no answer. Bonnie called information and got the number for the police in that town. An officer that answered the call told her that he was the first to arrive at the scene of the accident. Both individuals were at the point of impact. Tom was driving and Bonnie was in the rear seat behind him. The officer emphasized the fact that their deaths were instant, and was probably as pain-free as possible under the circumstances.

Two days after the accident, Emile and Bonnie had a visitor, the insurance agent in charge of investigating the accident and in settling the estate of Tom and Karen. Angela was the sole beneficiary. Whereas she was a minor, and an only child, the company had the responsibility of researching her legal guardians in case of the death of Tom and/or Bonnie. He informed them that an attorney that handled all of the company's legal transactions would be in touch with them shortly. The attorney, Walter Hatch, was located in Boston, Massachusetts.

It was difficult to keep the news from Angela. At some time she had to be told the truth. She knew that something had taken place because her Aunt Bonnie and Uncle Emile were upset about something. The attorney called them to make an appointment for the next day. They waited impatiently and put Angela in bed for a nap prior to the appointment time. She traditionally slept almost two hours before waking.

The lawyer arrived on time, and Tom quietly directed attorney Hatch to the large kitchen table. First, Mr. Hatch informed them that Angela was not the offspring of Tom and Karen. She was adopted!

Bonnie and Emile were shocked. "We never knew that she was adopted. Neither Tom nor Karen ever mentioned it to either of us," Emile explained. "Do you have any proof of that, Mr. Hatch?"

"Yes, I was the attorney who arranged the adoption. It's not unusual for the new parents to remain silent about an adoption. That way they can inform the child when they deem it appropriate, and the child is protected from hearing about his or her status from outside strangers, which can be devastating."

"We can understand that," Emile added.

The attorney searched his briefcase for some documents that would validate what he told them. "Normally, this information is never distributed to anyone other than the new parents. However, this is an unusual case where both parents are deceased and the child is a minor. The will that Tom and

Karen Huntley signed specified that you two were totally acceptable to them to raise Angela in case of their deaths."

"I can tell you that any information that you have disclosed to us will be held in strict confidence," Emile quickly stated. "I pledge that as an officer in the United States Army."

"I'm fully aware of your status in the Army, Colonel. You and your wife may study the document. Take your time." Mr. Hatch passed the documents to Emile.

He read them and quickly passed them on to Bonnie, getting out of his chair and walking about the kitchen. He was speechless.

She accepted them and cried out, "My God...it's unbelievable... When you came to Berlin did you know that Faye was our daughter, Mr. Hatch?"

"Yes, that was the main reason for my visit so that things could be settled as soon as possible. I cannot show you what the Huntleys stated, but I can tell you that it was a glowing recommendation that would make anyone proud. I think they made a wise decision for little Angela."

"Angela is sound asleep in the bedroom," Bonnie told him. "Are you going to take the child away from us?"

"I was going to ask the same question," Emile quickly added, still standing. "Let me be crystal clear, Mr. Hatch. Neither you nor anyone else is going to take this child away from us. If you take that statement as a threat, then so be it... That child is not going anywhere as long as I'm able to defend her rightful place in this crazy world, and for now she stays with us."

Walter Hatch pushed his chair away from the table and stood. "Colonel, you've made my day! My main purpose in coming here today as an agent for the adoption company was to determine what is best for the child. I have no authority to take the child from you! If you and your wife will be patient with me, I'll personally see to it that the proper documents are processed so that the child remains with you. I knew Tom and Karen well and am saddened by their sudden deaths. They were good people and would have given the child a good home. I'm convinced that you two will do the same. How fortunate it is that little Angela will not have to be disrupted and taken to total strangers at such an impressionable age. Maybe this is all a part of God's work and that your daughter will have a change of heart about the child she brought into this world. Who knows?... Miracles do happen."

"I've been thinking that very same thing, Sir," Bonnie exclaimed, overwhelmed by the events of the day."

"I was not anxious to make this trip," Mr. Hatch replied. "However, things have worked better than I anticipated. Paperwork will take a while, but I'll push it along as quickly as I can. God bless both of you. Little Angela will be saddened when she learns about her parents demise, but time will pass and she'll be happy with you two. I leave this beautiful portion of the White Mountains with a glad heart. Good-bye."

Emile and Bonnie were silent as they watched the attorney drive slowly down the road. Bonnie turned to her husband. "You know, Em, this period has given me more of a chance to observe Angela, and I've been amazed at how many things have reminded me of Faye as a baby. Especially her curly, blond hair and the little dimples on her cheeks. I never wanted to say anything to you because it would only hurt to talk about it."

"I, too, have seen those things, Bonnie. A couple of times I almost called her Faye when she went with me in the truck. Seeing her asleep on the seat with her head on my lap brought back a lot of memories. Today, we're witnessing right here in our home a miracle, Honey. I wonder how Faye is going to react to the news?"

"I was with her when the nurse took the baby from her. She had given birth to a beautiful child, and no mother gives up her child without experiencing some pain. She was truly traumatized, but she kept it to herself. I know that she shed a lot of tears. We should call to see how she's doing."

"That sounds like a good idea," Emile nodded in agreement.

Angela was standing in the doorway to the kitchen rubbing her sleepy eyes. Emile rushed to pick her up and embraced her. The Ranta family had just received a blessing from God in a very special way.

Bonnie was on the phone. "Hello, Faye? Your father and I were thinking about you and wondering what you were doing. School will soon be out for the year."

"I'm doing great, Mom. I have some special news to tell you and Dad. I've been seeing a very nice young man who is a math teacher here in Wells. He was wounded in the war and lost his hand on his left arm. He proposed to me last night, and I accepted."

"Honey, I'm so happy for you. You deserve someone special in your life. Living alone is no fun, and I speak from experience. Your father is doing well. We were wondering if you were busy this weekend. We could stop by and maybe have a meal at a good restaurant on the coast. We've never been to Warren's in Kittery."

"That sounds great, Mother. Bob Hansen has been anxious to meet the two of you. He was a Chief petty officer in the Navy and is a little apprehensive about meeting Dad, a colonel in the Army. I told him how great you both are."

"You know your dad," Bonnie answered. "He'll be proud to have a chief petty officer in the family."

"That's what I told Bob. I can't wait to show him off to you. We'll expect you this weekend."

Bonnie hung up the phone and looked into Emile's eyes. He was still holding Angela. "You heard the conversation. She's anxious to show off her new friend who proposed to her."

"That could complicate the surprise we're going to spring on her," Emile replied. "We'll just wait and see how things go.

Chapter Twenty Six

Emile was reluctant to inform Faye about Angela until they had received official confirmation from the adoption agency. He knew from experience that government red tape could easily foul things up. Even though attorney Hatch seemed capable of getting things done correctly, he suggested to Bonnie that they postpone their visit to Maine.

Bonnie thought about that for a moment and replied, "Well, Em, we don't have to reveal anything to Faye until things are finalized. I understand that. We should go to celebrate her engagement and confront her after we receive official acknowledgement of Angela's adoption to us."

"We could do that. We should also postpone telling Angela about the death of her parents. I'm not comfortable with deception, but it's probably the least hurtful way to handle it..."

"I agree, Em." Bonnie left her seat and embraced her husband. "The day that we renewed our vows to each other was the happiest day of my life. How proud I am of my husband. Forgive me for all the unhappiness I created over the years. I never appreciated it before, but now I understand how the men in your commands looked up to you for guidance when the going was difficult on the battlefield. I saw those same virtues in Alpha and Faye as they grew up and became adults. I pray that we're doing the right thing for Angela and Faye. Hold me, Em...hold me..."

They both agreed that silence was the best way for their visit to Maine. They made the trip as planned and were anxious to meet Faye's future husband, Robert Hansen. They were not disappointed. Bob Hansen was a quiet young man with good manners. He had earned his chief petty officer stripes in the Navy and had been seriously wounded by a Japanese suicide plane that hit the destroyer while he was directing gunfire of an anti-aircraft mount. Emile respected the chiefs in the Navy and the sergeants in the Army. They are the ones responsible for running the two services. He had always depended on his sergeants to get things done and was never disappointed.

Their seafood dinners at Warren's Restaurant in Kittery went smoothly. Angela seemed comfortable in the company of two men with an artificial arm and hand. Bob had a soft touch with children. He often kneeled down to speak to Angela and made her smile.

Several times during the course of the visit, Emile was aware that Faye was observing Angela closely. He had seen tears form in her eyes, and she quickly excused herself to go to the restroom. At that moment, Emile knew what she had been thinking about, and he wanted to tell her what had happened. Bonnie saw his concern for her and touched his arm as if to remind him of their agreement to wait for confirmation.

When it came time to leave, Emile hugged Faye and whispered in her ear, "I like the new man in your life, Faye. I think he's worthy of you."

"Thanks, Dad. Your approval is important for both of us. Drive carefully on the way home," Faye responded to his comments.

Bonnie embraced Bob before leaving and told him, "Thank you for making my daughter happy, Robert. She's a very special young lady." Then she turned to Faye, and spoke in a low voice. "I know that you still carry some guilt of things in the past, my dear daughter. Do not let that interfere with your engagement. Things have a way of working out, and I wish you and Bob all the best. I love you."

"I love you, too, Mom." It had been an emotional moment for them.

Bonnie placed Angela on the front seat between her and Emile with her head in her lap. It had been a nice visit and they were relieved that things went well. Angela soon fell asleep on the ride home, and Bonnie held her so that she would not fall off the seat if Emile had to stop quickly. She bent over her and kissed her on the cheek.

Emile saw her response and asked a question he had been thinking about since the attorney visited them. "Bonnie, when you hold Angela like you are now, what are your thoughts about her?"

"I'm not sure I know what you mean, Em."

"I mean do you see her as a potential mother or do you think of yourself as a grandmother?"

"Oh, Em, I don't think I can answer that right now. I'm filled with sadness for her... We should not discuss that until things become settled," she answered, holding Angela's hand in hers.

"I understand, Bonnie. It's going to be a long wait until we get confirmation. Do you need any groceries before we get home?"

"No, I stocked up on supplies the day you took Angela to work with you. It was nice to meet Bob. I'm happy for Faye. She deserves someone like him."

"I liked him, too. I'll bet he's a good teacher in the classroom."

Two weeks after their visit to Maine, Bonnie and Emile received official documentation that they were granted full custody of Angela. Attorney Hatch had phoned to congratulate them the same day they received the notice. Now they had to inform Angela of her new family status. She was entitled to the truth, and they were anxious to observe her reaction to the fact that the parents she grew up with and loved were no longer going to be with her. She was going to need a lot of love and affection if they were to replace Tom and Karen.

That night they sat her on the couch next to the fireplace and told her that her mother and father were in Heaven. They had been killed in an automobile accident. The most important fact that they wanted to impress upon her was that she was never going to be alone. They softly explained that her parents were in another world, but they would be with her in spirit and most likely would be her guardian angels. That seemed to make her feel better. She was a little young to understand all that had happened. She asked why they didn't say good-bye, and they explained that they had intended to return to take her home, but the accident prevented that.

The evening was filled with sadness, and Bonnie and Emile strongly emphasized that she had a home with them. A child that young would not feel the impact of her situation until some period of time passed. It was important for them to be sure that her days were as pleasant as possible, and that they truly conveyed the fact that they wanted her to live them. She knew that her father and Emile were good friends. Time was the only healer, and her new parents opened their hearts to the innocent child that had already become an important part of their lives.

The funeral for Tom and Karen was announced in a note from Karen's cousin. It was going to be in her home town. Emile wanted to attend the funeral. Tom had been a good friend, and he wanted to pay his respect to a courageous soldier who had faithfully followed him during the assault on Point du Hoc. He discussed it with Bonnie, and they agreed that Angela was too young to attend the funeral of her beloved parents, and Emile did not want to leave Bonnie alone with Angela if he did attend. He prayed for his friend and thanked God for the time they had fought together.

Winters in Northern New Hampshire can be severe, and the first snow arrived the week before Thanksgiving. They had invited Faye and Bob to celebrate the holiday and stay for a couple of days. Enough time had passed so that Angela seemed to adapt to her new home and seemed comfortable with Bonnie and Emile. It was also time that they inform Faye. They never told her that they had adopted Angela or that her parents had died in an auto accident. It was, without question, going to be a shock to her that this was her daughter. They were pleased that Bob would be present when Faye discovered the truth.

Anxiety filled the air at the log cabin when Thanksgiving arrived. Bonnie had enjoyed her role as a mother to Angela and was partially responsible for the child's remarkable response to the love that permeated the rustic cabin. Emile was concerned that when the time came for Faye to be told the truth, Bonnie might not be able to let her go! A strong bond had been built between the two during the weeks that they had been together. Emile, too, admitted that the child had won a place in his heart and he would miss her. However, he firmly believed that

Angela's rightful place was with her mother. It all depended on how Faye reacted to the truth...

Bob and Faye arrived at the cabin the day before Thanksgiving. They had driven in their brand new Studebaker Champion automobile. It was an attractive vehicle that set a standard for the rest of the postwar auto industry.

The moment Faye entered the cabin and saw Angela she was surprised and asked, "Are you still babysitting little Angela? I would think that Tom and Karen would want her for the holiday."

Emile saw that penetrating look in Faye's eyes and knew that something unusual had happened.

Bonnie looked at Emile and announced, "Em, I think it's time we told Faye and Tom."

"I agree," Emile replied. "We owe you and Bob an explanation and an apology. Please sit on the couch here beside the fireplace in the great room. Your mother and I owe you an explanation..."

"What in the world are you two talking about?" Faye impatiently cried, sitting on the couch.

Bonnie took a seat beside her and placed an arm about her shoulders. "Your Father and I took Angela while Bob and Karen went to a funeral in Kansas. They both were killed in an automobile accident on their return to New England."

"My God! How sad," Faye answered, satisfied that it explained Angela's presence. "She seems to be content with you two."

Emile backed up to the fireplace and clasped his hands behind him. He saw that Bob and Faye seemed satisfied with the explanation. He and Bonnie knew that Faye had told Bob about her pregnancy and adoption of her child.

He was prepared to tell them the full story when Faye asked "What's going to happen to Angela?"

Bonnie and Emile both searched for the right words. Bonnie stated firmly: "We've adopted Angela."

"You've adopted her...?"

"Yes," Emile quietly answered her question. "And that was when we discovered that Angela is the little girl that you gave birth to, Faye. Karen and Tom had adopted her. It has to be a work of God that the child is here now with her real mother and grandparents."

Faye leaped off the couch and began circling the room and cried out in anger, "You don't understand! I thought I had put that horrible experience behind me. Seeing Angela brings back all the ugly memories of that traumatic moment in my life." Faye fell in Bob's arms and wept. Despair filled the room.

"Neither of you knew the truth…" Faye screamed aloud, frightening Angela.

Bonnie felt helpless. "We're sorry that our actions have caused you such pain, Faye. Forgive us…"

"Honey," Emile tried to calm things down. "We never wanted to hurt you, but you became pregnant and gave the child up for adoption."

Faye again cried: "Neither of you understand me. I gave up the child because she was not a love child. She would always remind me of the most horrible experience of my life. The last time I visited you in Vermont, I was raped by your husband, Mom!"

The truth that Faye had been carrying alone for years was finally revealed. Bonnie rushed to take her in her arms. "I'm so sorry, Faye…I never knew…I never knew."

The loud, angry voices were making Angela very uncomfortable, and she began to cry, holding on to Emile. He picked her up and carried her into the kitchen, kissing her on the forehead. They should have waited until she was taking her afternoon nap. He understood now why Faye had been so angry with him when he first heard about her pregnancy.

Faye was an emotional wreck, releasing her mother and cried in Bob's arms. "I'm so sorry that you had to witness this, Bob. I think we should leave."

Bonnie broke down with tears streaming down her cheeks. This was no way to celebrate Thanksgiving. She did not want them to leave in anger. Just then, Emile walked back into the room with Angela in his arm. He, too, was concerned about their leaving.

"I think it's important that we reflect on this important time in our lives," Emile suggested in a calm voice. He looked directly at Faye. We had hopes that Angela's presence would be looked upon as an act of God. She's not responsible for all of the grief that fills this room. She's an innocent participant who cannot defend herself. I speak the truth when I tell you that this little four-year-old girl has touched our hearts, and we were anxious to share that joy with you, Faye. We were ignorant of the truth, and I admire your courage these past four years."

Tears filled Emile's eyes and Bonnie gently wiped them away with a handkerchief. "Angela deserves to live in a home filled with love such as she had with Karen and Tom. Your mother and I had hoped that you would welcome her into the family where she rightly belongs. Like it or not, Faye, you gave her life…"

The room was quiet and filled with emotion. Angela hugged Emile and looked at Faye. Somehow, she knew that the lady who had been crying had been studying her with tear stained eyes. She released her grip on Emile's head and reached out to Faye saying in a strained voice: "Are you angry at me?"

Unable to control herself, Faye took her in her arms and cried; "No, Angela, I'm not angry at you, I'm your mother!!"

Postscript - Defender of Freedom

The popular British singer of the World War II period, Vera Lynn, touched the hearts of soldiers from every country in the world. She was the personification of everything noble, decent, and worthwhile that the soldiers were fighting for. For a short period of time, she became the symbol of home, family, and loved ones left behind. With the voice of an angel, she drew tears from battle-weary soldiers manning outposts in a foreign land far from home.

Frightened, weary, and lonely, they were softened by her renditions of popular songs: *The White Cliffs of Dover, We'll Meet Again,* and other moving ballads of the period, remained with the young Americans long after they returned home and began raising their families. The haunting refrains became an integral part of their war experience. Her soft voice sent a message of hope for a better tomorrow. She remained popular with the veterans for years after the war.

Memories of her gentle voice with a British accent became a treasured symbol of that monumental period in the lives of the young veterans a long ways from home in a foreign land. Even today, over seventy years later, the lovely lady's songs have the power to inflame old memories and can still produce a tear in the eyes of an aged veteran who remembers. No other voice touched the hearts of the lonely soldiers the same way. All of her songs were an emotional experience, but *We'll Meet Again,* was special. It began: "We'll meet again, don't know where, don't know when..."

How could they ever forget?

The End

Other Historical Romance Novels
BY
Clifton LaBree

A Song for Lisa   A Historical Romance

This is the story of a young American woman captured by the Japanese in the Philippines, 1941. Like most prisoners, she was brutalized and sadistically treated with a cruel disregard for human life. Three years later, Lisa and her companions had reached the low point of starvation and abuse .....

Lake of Three Sorrows   A Historical Romance

A warm spiritually uplifting story of courage, commitment, and sacrifice. This is the story of Dale Cooper, a battle-weary American soldier who served in two world wars.

Flickering Flame (Colonial Series Book One)

A historical novel, about the Cullen family who settled in Portsmouth, New Hampshire, and their participation in events prior to the French and Indian War. Freedom and opportunity were on the march, but it extracted a heavy price. Frontier settlers were ruthlessly killed and butchered by rampaging Indians lead by French officers and Jesuit priests who frequently incited them to greater levels of inhumanity...

Raising the Torch (Colonial Series Book Two)

A continuation of the saga from Flickering Flame, Colonial Series book one, of the Cullen family in Colonial Portsmouth. This is a moving story of love and sacrifice when a small colony had the audacity to fight for independence from their motherland...

Non-Fiction Books

By

Clifton LaBree

New Hampshire's General John Stark,

Live Free or Die: Death Is Not the Greatest of Evils

Published by - Fading Shadows Imprint

A fresh look at one of America's staunchest defenders of liberty and freedom. John Stark was a courageous New Hampshire citizen-soldier who fought in both, the French and Indian War, and the Revolutionary War. His pursuit of leadership excellence on the battlefield distinguished him as one of the most successful combat commanders of the war, and one of the least appreciated.

His selflessness, modest life style, and devotion to the cause of freedom are an inspiration that time has not diminished. He remains today the embodiment of the frugal, independent, and cantankerous New Hampshire Yankee.

Gentle Warrior, General Oliver Prince Smith, USMC

Published by - Kent State University Press. Kent, Ohio, 2001

The Story of one of the United States Marine Corps best General Officer. His flawless performance in Korea is a story that needed to be told.

FADING SHADOWS IMPRINT

Fading Shadows Imprint was established to bring to the public books of historical events and portraits of people enduring tragic circumstances of by-gone days. Hopefully, they will generate a deep appreciation and respect for the exceptionalness of the United States of America, and an appreciation for the sacrifice and selflessness of those who valiantly served for liberty and freedom.

The characters are fictional, but the historical events and dates have been seriously researched and are factually presented. Some books feature incidents during the French and Indian Wars as well as the War for Independence.

World Wars I and II are eras rich in stories that beg to be told. I've tried to pay tribute to the collective courage and heroism, often unheralded, that has defined Americans in every engagement. It was a time when the immortality of dreams and aspirations were defended by the blood of young men and women. There is a beautiful monument and cemetery in a small French village where thousands of white crosses and Stars-of-David are set in perfect alignment, honoring thousands of American soldiers who gave their last full measure. A large granite slab bearing mute witness to their sacrifice has the following words chiseled in stone: TIME WILL NOT DIM THE GLORY OF THEIR DEEDS. Another monument reads: VIRTUE AND COURAGE ARE THEIR OWN MONUMENT AND REWARD. Those simple words define the American soldier from the dark days of the Revolutionary War to the present. They are an American treasure, unique in the history of the world.

Every generation has its own signature and characteristics that uniquely define them. The World War II generation is defined by the immortality of the ideals and truth they gallantly defended.

The United States has freely given precious blood and treasure to defend the rights of man to be free, and we have never asked for anything in return. No other nation on the planet has sacrificed so much for the noble virtues of liberty and freedom. We hope that the selections offered by Fading Shadows Imprint will touch your hearts and generate a deeper appreciation and love for our country.